HIGHWAY 101

Books by Harrison Edward Livingstone

Novels

> *David Johnson Passed Through Here*
> *HARVARD, John*
> *The Wild Rose*
> *Baltimore*
> *The Agent*
> *Redbeard The Pirate*
> *Big Sur and the Canyon*
> *This Autumn*
> *Marcie*
> *Highway 101*
> *Camping Out*
> *Kim*

On the assassination of John F. Kennedy

> *High Treason*
> *High Treason 2*
> *Killing the Truth*
> *Killing Kennedy*
> *The Radical Right and the Murder of President John F. Kennedy:*
>   *Stunning Evidence in the Assassination of the President*
> *The Hoax of the Century: Decoding the Forgery of the Zapruder Film*

Films:
The American Revolution Collected Best Films, Vols. II, III, IV

PLAYS:
Collected Best Plays, Vols I & II

Short Stories and Poems

HIGHWAY 101

A Novel By
Harrison Edward Livingstone

iUniverse, Inc.
New York Lincoln Shanghai

HIGHWAY 101

Copyright © 2006 by Harrison Edward Livingstone

All rights reserved. No part of this book may be used or reproduced by any means, graphic, electronic, or mechanical, including photocopying, recording, taping or by any information storage retrieval system without the written permission of the publisher except in the case of brief quotations embodied in critical articles and reviews.

iUniverse books may be ordered through booksellers or by contacting:

iUniverse
2021 Pine Lake Road, Suite 100
Lincoln, NE 68512
www.iuniverse.com
1-800-Authors (1-800-288-4677)

ISBN-13: 978-0-595-38771-7 (pbk)
ISBN-13: 978-0-595-83153-1 (ebk)
ISBN-10: 0-595-38771-3 (pbk)
ISBN-10: 0-595-83153-2 (ebk)

Printed in the United States of America

Some people naturally ruin their lives. Others have it messed up for them. Quite a few people and professions take advantage of the most vulnerable people. Corruption runs far deeper than most people ever realize, but all life and society is demoralized by it.

Chapter 1

▼

January, 1975

Peter Casey's car left 101 with its four lanes, divider strips, shoulders, huge signs, big trucks, chain link fences, and the purple haze of poisoned air, and headed toward the coastal mountains on an old road.

The Jolon Road passed among alfalfa fields and a few oil wells, then hills and pastures where cattle fattened. The mountains loomed in the West, and on the other side was the Pacific. Six thousand feet of rugged and impassible terrain straight up, pushed skyward by the collision of sea and continent, they say, of two tectonic plates. How very different were those few miles to the sea from the Salinas Valley with its broad, rich and flat fields hot and dry in the summer, to the mysterious and magic place among the mountains where no one lived but a few isolated ranchers. At first there were only some green California oaks spotted across the fields and hills. There were more oak trees as he drove closer to the mountains. Great forests were there, of redwood and madrone, ponderosa, California oak, sycamore, and Coulter Pine. Santa Lucia Fir stood on the slopes of Cone Peak—very rare trees.

On the other side of the ridge was Big Sur, the magical place of Robinson Jeffers and Henry Miller, exposed to the raw winter storms of the Pacific, raging and blowing, raining, snowing. Seals, whales, and sea otters plied the chill currents, and fogs and winds blowing off the nearby Alaska current froze the mountainsides falling to the sea.

After resting a few days, Peter drove over the Coast Ridge on the Nacimiento-Ferguson Road after the long, two month trip from New York in the dead of winter in his old car, through Montana, Wyoming, Colorado, Texas. He came down to the sea and felt the salt and the wind on his face.

What a sight to come over the saddle on the ridge and get that first look at the Pacific from nearly a mile high five miles back from the ocean's edge, looking out to the horizon fifty miles at ships far out in the mists!

His VW Bug's odometer showed 7500 miles since leaving Manhattan. Far away was Lincoln Center and the New York City Ballet, Pamala Tate, his kitchen and little apartment on 105th Street. Seventy-five hundred miles, the distance from Vladivostok to Moscow or Warsaw, perhaps. A long, long way. He would miss the ballet in the Wilderness...And so many plays.

How tired Peter was. His small survival kit—his car—rolled on quietly, across the range land, through the brown oats and pastures of Hunter Liggett Military Reservation toward the Los Padres, so soon to be destroyed—for a time—by fire. Some heavy army tanks stood among the trees, their long ugly, deadly cannons pointed at the squirrels. Woe unto them!

It was January when his arduous journey ended, and he came down to the San Antonio River. It was just a stream in the woods, but as far as he was going, for now. He had to camp there until something broke. The stream was too deep for his car, but a four wheel drive could get across.

He knew that his car engine was damaged, but it might last awhile, until some money came. The valves that had been replaced in Texas with Mexican heads were nothing but soft lead and had gone bad again. He had no compression. The valves had burned out in Montana, and he had an engine job for $500 in Austin, borrowing the money. They forgot to replace the heater hoses and the car broke down after two hundred miles, and he nearly froze in a blizzard out on the desert going to El Paso. Later the car got as far as Phoenix and he begged and borrowed more money on the long distance telephone to save it. He was a week in Texas begging and a week in Phoenix begging, then headed West to where he hoped it was warmer and where he could camp.

His emotions were shattered.

Peter had only a few dollars, and a couple of boxes of groceries his cousin had bought for him. The nation was in a deep business recession, and unemployment in California was past ten percent. The auto assembly lines closed down, the factories silent, people frightened, the lines of the unemployed grown very long. The public had revolted and stopped buying the big gas-eating American cars. Used car lots stood overflowing with huge guzzlers with tremendous overhangs and lots of chrome. Ah, how he wished he had one of those monster tanks, one of the last of the great muscle cars. At least they were big enough to sleep in, laid out in the back seat.

Peter was hounded from place to place and often he did not know where to go next, where to run. All the joy and good works he had been capable of departed like the soul of a dead man leaving his body. He lived in terror, unable to smile for long periods of time. Life, without love or purpose, lost its meaning.

They treated him badly, as though he were an impostor. "Who is this guy?" people wanted to know.

"He's on the run."

"Nobody must want him."

"Must be in trouble somewhere."

"That can't be his real name."

"A guy like that, with a background like that—there's something funny there...."

"What do you suppose he did?"

"Shouldn't be broke. He's got no place to stay, no home. Must be in some kind of trouble."

"People get what they deserve in life."

"God is punishing him."

"Maybe he's a secret agent of some kind." He was, in a way.

If a person dressed in sack cloth and ashes is a test from God—that is—if the poor and unemployed come to the door of the secure and fat needing a handout or help, it is a test from powers far greater than us. "There but for the Grace of God go I...." his father always used to say.

Peter had no sense of place any longer, no home, nowhere to go. He sometimes lost hope and wanted to die. For surely they meant to kill him.

The trouble began long before, long before he had a sworn enemy, a man who said that he would destroy him, and yet Peter never understood why.

The trouble stemmed from trying to live life on his own terms. That was an unforgivable sin. But he was closed off, without knowing it, from further progress, from any success. What they did to him was in a smaller way what they did to President Kennedy. They did it to a lot of people. But it was more torturous for many than a quick bullet exploding your skull. It was slow death.

John Kennedy was still alive when Peter joined the Peace Corps. Tens of thousands of young people answered the President's call to do something for their country, for the world, for peace. Peter was one of them.

The CIA and military intelligence was right there, from the beginning of the Peace Corps, subverting, using. There were fifty men in his group, all of them veterans. His roommates were military intelligence operatives from Indochina. They did not really appear to have been separated from the Marines, and were under cover. The leader of the group was a "retired" colonel in the Marines. He was from Texas, and he hated "niggers," but he was going to take this group to Gabon, in Africa. All those Peace Corps groups with wholesome young American girls from Indiana and Iowa were just a show and diverted attention from what was really going on.

The President didn't want this, but he did not know it was happening until other nations exposed the CIA or DIA in the Peace Corps, and some of the groups were expelled very publicly. But Americans often heard nothing about it. Sometimes it was in the news when they could not hide the charges. The charges were presented to the country in such a way that they didn't believe it. Only radicals believed it.

The President was betrayed at the Bay of Pigs, and he fired the top command of the CIA. "I will smash the CIA into a thousand pieces," he said. But they got him back.

Peter was training in Puerto Rico when the President's young brother, Edward Kennedy, came down to see them. Peter found some time to talk with Senator Kennedy. "This group," he said, "is a CIA and military operation."

"It is?"

"Take a good look at it."

"All right."

"Every man in this group was—or is—in the service."

"What do you mean *in the service?*"

"I think they are still on active duty, under cover."

"Really?!"

They talked for some time and the Senator had Peter photographed with him. The picture was on the front page of every paper in the world, and in *Life*. "Tell your brother, Peter said.

That's when he made himself a target. He made the mistake of blabbing what he had seen to the wrong people when he left and went home.

Years after, when he quarried Harris Wofford, later to be Senator Harris Wofford, there was no record of the group ever having existed. Wofford had been one of the leaders of the Peace Corps.

Were they all dead? All fifty men? Or just non persons? They were down the memory hole.

Some of these Peace Corps outfits were exposed then, and expelled from their host country. Peter quit after a few months and went home. He made the mistake of telling a friend, an attorney, that the group was CIA. The attorney had been in the OSS and helped form the CIA. He was in the Power Control Group. He knew Chuck Colson and Howard Hunt among Richard Nixon's henchmen. Nixon was deeply involved in planning the Bay of Pigs operation. Nixon hated Kennedy for not backing up the operation with a big invasion. Kennedy defeated Nixon in the 1960 election and Nixon hated him for it.

"...We can't afford to make a mistake in America. So, if this young Kennedy makes a mistake, he's got to be impeached immediately. We can't wait for a second," Henry Luce said. He owned Time and Life.

At the time Peter was in the Peace Corps, Robert Kennedy said, "We are under pressure from our military to use force against Cuba.... If the situation continues much longer, the President is not sure that the military will not overthrow him and seize power." There was such a conspiracy during the presidency of Franklin Delano Roosevelt.[1]

Peter was marked from that moment. Attorneys, as officers of the Court, are there to control us. Especially if somebody is a teacher, writer, journalist or free lance. These professions influence public opinion, and they must be controlled.

From that time on Peter never had a decent job, never had a fair chance. Everything he touched slipped from his hands like sand. He undertook years of study, worked his ass off and took degrees in night school, and it was all for nothing. He had no hope. They would utterly destroy him. He had to find another way to win through.

One of the most difficult lessons in life is the fact that some people, in order to cover up for their mistakes, will fabricate the cause of the trouble and blame someone else for their own failure. They will even attempt to destroy the evidence—ruining the victim. Ruining their mind and life.

The stream was full from winter rains. It was two feet deep and 25 feet across. The water was very cold, but good to drink. Pure. It was free of chemicals. The air, too, was pure, and washed by the Pacific just over the mountains, twenty miles away. There were certain advantages of being an outcast—at least for brief periods of time.

The stream rushed over the rocks with the force of the torrents that had fallen, glistening in the sun, making a pleasant, lulling noise.

Peter got into his car and backed it in among the trees, out of sight, and returned to the stream, a few feet away. He stood for a time, then watched himself wind down, knowing that the winter-long journey was at an end and he would stay there until Spring. He got out his pipe and buttoned up his jacket against the cold, smoked the pipe and listened to the rushing stream. Nothing could have been nicer, for the time being.

The world had been suckered into sensate pleasure, the momentary hedonism of manufactured pleasures. The highest pleasure was that of the

---

1. The "Smedley Butler Affair", told in a small book about General Butler, USMC, which contains his own article, "War Is A Racket" (the title of the book).

spirit when it soared above the moment. He longed for something more, something beyond this veil of tears, and he learned to find pleasure in the moment, to find joy away from cities and polluted air, to forget what they were doing to him. And to others. There was an answer somewhere, for himself, and for mankind. Maybe. Before it was too late.

An answer to loneliness. He couldn't stay there forever, and he couldn't leave the city for too many months.

God, what have they done to our youth, to our nation? The Police State was surely here, he was beginning to find out. *1984.* "Who controls the past controls the future," George Orwell wrote in *1984.*

Some birds went about their business. A little distance away he spotted a few deer grazing quietly in a sunny spot among the trees.

Yes, they had gone around the city, those men from Edgewood Arsenal, drugged the young people in the bars, dropping LSD in people's drinks, hooking people on heroin and pot, the U.S. Army did, looking for new conquests, having been beaten abroad, they would conquer us and the squirrels, destroy all the young men, the best men of his generation. Yet another generation of young men and women and their creativity destroyed and enslaved. Someone else would decide what we would build and how the world would be. Not the people. If it wasn't the Germans or the Japs or the Russians, it was ourselves. *We* are the enemy.

That was democracy and that was a frightening prospect: being governed by the mob.

After awhile Peter got up from his rock and went to the car. He found his tent and set it up on a level bit of sand, driving the steel pegs in deep with a small rock. It was large enough to just sit up inside, and had room for two to sleep. But there was only one of him. In Sri Lanka, nobody ever slept alone, from birth to death.

"Here I stay," he said aloud. He put his foam mattress, sleeping bag and pillow, a small blanket, a heavy coat, and a flashlight inside the tent. Then he set up the small folding sterno stove, opened a can of baked beans, and another of Vienna sausage, and put it into his mess kit. Plenty of pepper and garlic powder. It was evening and the sun came down low over the mountains leaving him in long shadow. Far overhead a jet plane left its sunlit white contrails across the sky. He was too tired to gather wood and make a fire pit with rocks.

It was very quiet there. He could hear the occasional crackle of the burning sterno, and time slowed down and nearly stopped. The bean gravy began to bubble. He stirred the food and put in pepper again, and covered it.

There was a small can of apple juice to go with dinner, and a piece of cheese. When the sun was down and it grew dark, the cold of night set in. The temperature dropped below freezing. He made hot chocolate and had an oatmeal cookie by the light of a candle lantern.

He felt the chill set in, and bundled up more.

Peter finished dinner and sat in the car and found some classical music: Radio Reno, Nevada, and Zubin Mehta and the Los Angeles Philharmonic doing overtures from Wagner and other war horses. It'll do, he thought, snobbishly, thinking of the big Eastern symphony orchestras of haughty fame. He lit his pipe and opened some red wine and took a slug, starring into the darkness ahead through the windshield of his VW, long ago remembering Rebecca and sitting in that same car, close, listening to the rain on the steel womb around them, on Linnean Street at Radcliffe.

It was a spooky place, dark, alone, fifty miles from town.

Peter drank up several cups of wine while he listened to the music on his car radio, and got loaded that first night alone in the forest he knew so well. He began to plan a backpack trip into the interior. The drinking felt good. When the evening was over he turned off the radio and went out for a walk in the cold air to piss. It was real cold, below freezing, and the grass was frosted. The dark presence of the trees stood close in the blackness. It was still and quiet, except for the sound of the stream a few yards away, and the far off howl of a coyote. The Moon came up and lit the primeval landscape. He walked for awhile, and then unzipped his tent and closed himself in for the night, using the candle lantern. The ground was cold and hard. In the morning, he would gather leaves and pine needles and make a soft bed under the tent.

The candle seemed to take the chill off. He could see his breath. It got down to ten degrees that night. He kept a heavy coat over his sleeping bag and slept in his clothes, with a sweater on, and an old navy watch cap on his head, burying his face and head inside the sleeping bag.

It was fine to stretch out on the ground after so many miles of driving. For a long time he lay awake, sometimes uncovering his head and staring out through the window in the tent over his head, at the sky, at the moonlight on the trees.

Somehow he would get free. Maybe he was becoming free. He was free of being a robot and programming—what they did to everyone else—at least for now. And yet, he saw.... he *was* programmed, angry, frustrated, afraid. How to get free and have complete control over his destiny? People had to work to survive.

It was hell taking a piss during the night—getting up very stiff, and crawling out through the small tent's door into the freezing air.

The next day illiterate rednecks came out and shot off their guns and got drunk, littering the pristine forest with beer cans, food wrappers, and empty ammunition boxes. They were going to save America, and shoot up the "long hairs" and hippies and Beatniks when America ran out of gas and oil. They were taking names like a lot of radical cops.

Peter kept a low profile and they didn't notice him close by in the woods. When they were gone, Peter picked up their litter and saved it for kindling to get his campfires going.

Oh, yes, and the squirrels, too, were a big problem for the Army. The squirrels were undermining their new electronic battlefield and the Army couldn't have that. The battle raged from the Santa Lucias to the Pentagon. "They are a health threat," the Army said, as they prepared to use sodium flouroacetate (compound 1080). "They may harbor bubonic plague." There were millions of squirrels there eating up the battlefield, like an infestation in a pin ball machine. Maybe billions of squirrels also threatening the soldiers, apparently. No cases of bubonic plague were reported yet. Ever. The Army wanted an exception to Executive Order

11870 forbidding the use of poisons on Federal land that can be passed from one animal to another.

"However, Representative G. William Whitehurst (R-Va.), a member of the House Armed Services Committee, has asked President Ford not to allow the exception because he thinks that using the Chemical would be like using the atomic bomb.

"A single ounce of 1080 can kill more that 200 humans.

"Also involved are the California Department of Health, the Fish and Wildlife Service, the Monterey Country agricultural commissioner, cattle ranchers, environmentalists, the Interior Department, the Agriculture Department, and the Environmental Protection Agency, along with the Army and Congress." They forgot the Sierra Club.

Strange that the public didn't know about it. The cattlemen have been shooting the coyotes that ordinarily eat the squirrels. "The resulting gain in chipmunk population is nature speaking back," said Whitehurst. "I hope the Army directs some attention to the problems of overgrazing and the drastically reduced predator population in the region.

"Squirrels are attracted to heavily grazed land because they rely on being able to see as a defense against predators. If the land were not as heavily grazed, the result would be fewer squirrels. Then the Sierra Club said that 1080 was not only highly effective in killing ground squirrels but is violently toxic to other wildlife as well, both directly and indirectly, both game and non-game. And the Sierra Club demanded that the Army file an environmental impact report on possible effects of the proposed 1080 campaign. Victor Veysey, assistant secretary of the Army for Civil Works, stated the program would be put off until completion of such a study by the Department of the Interior.

"The Army estimates there are seven to 10 million squirrels at Hunter Liggett alone. But John Davis said that medical data indicate so few people have contracted the disease there is little need for such a widespread poisoning program. So the Army says that there are other problems. The squirrels 'chewed up an earthen dam at Liggett and made the dam collapse,' an Army spokesman said. 'They burrowed under the edge of an airport runway and made the paving sink. They even stick their heads up through paved roads. Farmers have also complained the little animals attack their land and eat their crops.'

"The Army spokesman said the squirrel population began to mushroom in 1971 after President Nixon issued the chemical ban on federal land. Briefly, the Army allowed unlimited hunting of the animals.

"The Army said some grazing at Hunter Liggett is necessary to prevent fires when trainees use tracer bullets and other equipment that is part of the 'automated battlefield' the Army is trying to develop there.

"But the growth of the squirrel population is diminishing. 'There are only about one-third as many young ones this year as last. This is because there is so little food for them. This is partly a function of grazing and partially a function of drought. There are also some of the skinniest cows you've ever seen out there. About as skinny as the squirrels,' said Katy Newbold, a graduate student in ecology currently doing research on the squirrels at Hunter Liggett."

Well, they had one more squirrel gone underground there, in his tent, getting ready to undermine things. But maybe they would get him first. The United States Army had an ongoing problem with critters it was unable to defeat.

Chapter 2

▼

"The American attitude is that of the economically rational man: If these people are willing to be shafted, then I will shaft them. If I can bribe or force or manipulate them to my advantage, I will. Since we in the United States have a stronger culture, then we will shaft them."

—Samuel del Villar

He knew psychological terror, and it was defeating him. It was not possible to remain positive when he was a target for destabilization and control, for destruction. He was in the *first circle*, but he was alone, with nothing to back him up, and nothing for a point of reference. Fear and horror overwhelmed him. But only he could know what was happening to him, what they were doing to him. No one else could know or understand. He was cast down like a pariah dog. Cast out. Marked for destruction.

He had fought them hard, and would fight them again. He was a dissenter. An American dissenter.

But Peter was no Red. No radical at all. He was in the Center. He was an American. The people he was up against were the radicals.

They had the Power. How could the conflict be reconciled?

Peter remained in his camp for a number of weeks. No one came by except for the first group of beer can and bottle target shooters. He went out every ten days for supplies, and drove over to the Coast to bathe at the hot springs late at night, when he could sneak in. Soon his unemployment checks came through. Lucky.

Snow came, and it was very cold in his tent at night. He read and studied a great deal, and built a small fire pit to stay warm. He remained in touch with the outside world on the car radio. He tried to figure out what to do and how to get a job. He could not raise enough money to rent a place anywhere long enough to find work. His body was injured, and it would be hard to do any work at all. He knew that as soon as he found work, *they* would find him, and he would lose the job. Things would start happening to him. He was afraid to take a job, afraid to even look. He was afraid of the things that happened to him over the last six years on jobs, of being trapped where they wanted him, where they could do things to him.

They wanted him on the run. Most people were eventually defeated once they ran. In his last job in New York, he had been punched. They had asked him to falsify a medical study—asked to compromise everything he believed in. He did not do it. Think about a country where doctors falsify medical reports, rig research projects, suppress, for instance, the results of a study that found that a main cause of leukemia are diagnostic X-rays...A lot of this happens.

It seems to be in the best interests of the medical industrial complex to keep diseases going, in fact, perhaps, generate them. It seems to be in the interests of the muscular dystrophy associations or the multiple sclerosis associations or the cancer outfits to suppress the research of their own or others that might help or even cure victims. The government moneys and private charitable groups go to the mediocre, to those without answers, who will have no answers, and funds are withdrawn from those scientists who have an answer. In not too subtle ways it is suggested to them that grants will be available for non controversial work.

And if you want a grant for a truly important project, lie about what you're going to use if for. Deceit is built into the system.

Is a medical establishment that operates this way any different from those criminal doctors in war who experimented on *untermensh*? On people?

He got a job working in a heart research project and was beaten up when he started to ask questions and get into locked files. It took several years before he was vindicated, when what they had tried to cover up came out. That famous teaching hospital was hiding treadmill tests that showed the negative side of coronary artery transplants at the time. The government was trying to check on them. Peter was the looser for discovering the truth. But getting the truth to the authorities was all but impossible because he was thrown out so fast. But, he did get the news out. And paid for it.

It was a coronary artery surgery transplant study conducted by the government at some university hospitals. The hospital that hired him must have figured he was a normal person, and had no morals. The government wanted to know if the huge increases in the cost of medical insurance caused by the new operation were justified. Somebody wanted to know if the operation worked.

But the study was co-opted at the start by the same profiteering doctors in the cardiology departments with whom they contracted.

The doctors had been excited when they were chosen for the study because they saw some new income for their department and for themselves. They saw a chance to co-opt the deal and steer it the way they wanted, covering up the facts.

Years later, the results came out. The operation helped some people, but did not help as many as they claimed. It was a business, like other operations in the medical industry, like hysterectomies and appendectomies. Often unnecessary.

It was a business, like high priced tests would later become.

So, of course, the hospitals conducting the study had to falsify some of the results. They did that by locking up their records and preventing Peter from seeing them on his own. He saw only what they wanted to show him. They did not show too many cases where patients failed the treadmill. Or died on the treadmill. The hospital where Peter worked locked up their treadmill results, and only handed Peter what they wanted him to now.

"You've got to get in there when she's at lunch," a doctor told Peter, on the Q.T.

"But the files are locked."

"The key is in her desk drawer."

He felt set up. Hilda the treadmill operator was 6'2" and may have had former employment as a guard in Auschwitz. She was a tough diesel dyke.

He knew that he had been located. He shot himself down. He was on the phone one day with a literary agent. "Where do you work?" the man asked. If he could be properly called a "man."

He had asked Peter several times before. Peter slipped and told him this time. He needed him. "St. Andrew's hospital," he said.

Soon it became apparent that a call had been made to the hospital. A chill set in. They probably told them he was a drug addict and would steal drugs from them. Things started to go wrong. His pay was cut, but he did not notice that at first. People started to talk badly to him. They treated him like dirt.

He got caught by Hilda, the treadmill operator, when he was in her files. Of course, the doctor who put him up to it knew he was in there that day. He had, in a previous raid on the files, found many cases that had not been shown to him, and they were all negative. That is, they showed that the expensive operation hadn't done a damn bit of good.

"What are you doing?"

"Just looking in the files." Hilda did not hesitate, but slugged him. No one saw it. He went to the head doctor, the chief of the department. That was a mistake.

"Hilda slugged me."

"I can't believe that! I don't believe you. You're lying." So that was where it was at.

"I swear to you, she slugged me."

"We understand that you are a violent character. We were told that you hit her, and that you have had quite a bit of trouble before you came here. I'm sorry, but I'm going to have to let you go."

"You're not sorry!" Stunned, Peter found his way out, but took all of his records, work, and files with him, and made a long report to the people in Seattle who were running the study. He also sent copies to the NIH in Washington.

Seattle was lucky because *they* were straight, and had warned Peter in advance that the study might be rigged. He knew what to look for: missing treadmill records.

The good doctors—some of the nation's most respected—got him first. He applied for unemployment benefits, and found that he could not get it.

After waiting weeks he was told, "You were fired. You are denied unemployment compensation." Fortunately, he had some savings and lived on that while he was driving and camping.

So, getting a little better at fighting back, Peter put the arm on the head doctor. He sent him documented proof that he was conducting a crooked study. Back came a letter to him:

"Dear Mr. Casey:

Your letter of October 3 to Dr. Harris was referred to me. The following actions have been taken:

(1) I called the Manager of the New York State Unemployment Office where you applied for benefits. I stated that a further investigation of your separation had indicated that you were not discharged for misconduct and would therefore, in my opinion, be eligible for benefits.

(2) A letter was sent to the Manager of the Unemployment Office stating the contents of item (1) above.

The New York State Unemployment Office informs us that it is unable to make a determination of your claim because it cannot obtain adequate information from your out-of-state employers.

Sincerely, /S/

If you want something, you have to fight for it. He had never collected unemployment compensation before, but this time he wanted it because he wanted to write a book. He had paid enough into the fund.

His previous employer, out-of-state, was the U.S. Government. Naturally, *they* did not want to pay the cost of his writing a book, or surviving, and so they had been careful to fire him for misconduct, too, although he did not know that was what they had done. That is, they put in his records that he had been fired for misconduct. This is how people get framed so that the law is evaded.

So he could never get another job with the government. Getting the first one was an accident anyway. Somebody slipped up. They were already building a case that would forever prevent him from getting any work. Things that had happened six years before would see to that. But somehow, now and then, he found a little job for a little while.

Chapter 3

The previous year, he had been living in the East, and out of a job, and when a letter came from Bill, a U.S. Forest ranger friend in California that he could use Peter to help clear trail:

"Dear Peter,

We've had a lot of snow here, about four feet. The whole forest is broken—every tree killed or damaged. The trails are blocked with fallen timber. If you can come out here, I'll get you hired. Get some new hiking boots and Forest Service uniforms, and you can help me clear trail. So be ready...."

Peter needed a job so badly, even for the minimum wage, that he wrote back and asked: "Can they really pay me?" He had done trail clearance as a volunteer long enough!

"Yes," came the reply. "Come out and be ready. You'll probably be working with me." Peter wanted nothing better than to go into the back country with him.

The letter told him what uniforms and boots to buy, and Peter spent one hundred dollars to get what was needed. The letter was like a fresh breeze and filled with hope. He hauled out a stack of fine color photographs and showed them to his girlfriend, a student at Barnard. The pictures showed the beauty of that National Forest and its mountains, before a series of terrible fires all but destroyed it. Peter showed Pamala the tall redwoods and mountains, long stretches of trail deep in the silent forest. It was plain to see that he loved that place.

Peter had worked in the forest as a volunteer off and on for several years. He took to helping the ranger do his job, and learned to handle the stock, saddle up and load the mules, and bed the animals down at night. He liked it better out there in the good clean air than in any city.

He dug holes for outhouses and helped put together new ones to replace those which people had chopped up for firewood. Of course, they were only a box over the hole in the ground, with a hole to sit over and shit through.

He helped put in stoves and new grates, repair picnic tables, and cut fallen trees across the trail, clear overgrown places on the trails, and pick up garbage from some of the camps that got littered up. He thought of that forest as his garden, and was always tinkering with it, and would clear a trail entirely on his own, without asking anyone. He had his own pruning shears for that purpose. He did this part of each summer for several years.

One year, the Forest Service decided that the sense of the Wilderness Act was that there would be no more picnic tables or stoves in the wilderness areas of the national forests. So the rangers, particularly the more countrified among them, gleefully went through the camps chopping up and burning the $800 redwood picnic tables. They ripped out the stoves, too. Let the sparks fly! Fire was good and "cleansed" the forest. It was natural. So what if it barbecued a few campers and deer and caused mud slides that took down stands of 5000 year old redwoods!

Up to that time, anyone building a fire outside of the campgrounds, or anywhere in a ring of stones and not in a stove, was subject to a fine. They conned everyone into believing that the threat of fire was greater. Then, all of a sudden, it was okay to build a fire anywhere in the wilderness area, in a fire ring.

What kind of a deal is this, he thought, when he saw the chopped up redwood tables. Anyone who cuts a redwood tree ought to be shot, and the same for tables.

His friend, the ranger, did not care for a desk job in one of the ranger stations. Nor did he seem to desire advancement. He was non political. The ranger stuck to the back-country where he dealt only with back-packers, horses, mules, deer and whatever other animals there were in the area. Of course, a few people lived in the area at the Avila Ranch, near Jolon, and on the Coast Ridge Road.

Bill was a fine man. He got along with the "long hairs" and "hippies" and defended them to the "short hairs" who were his bosses. Eventually, the Forest Service, or Congress, or somebody, maybe God, made the local bosses hire part time summer help. What a shock it was to see young men with beards, girls, and retired folks in green Forest Service uniforms doing a good job out there. Rednecks had always controlled it before.

There was a disastrous winter one year. Four feet of snow fell where there was ordinarily little if any snow. For fifty miles the devastation in the mountains was very great, and the sides of the mountains were brown with dead trees and fallen branches. Entire stands of tall Coulter Pine were broken off at the base, as though cut with a giant scythe, and laid down flat. It was pitiful to see, for someone who loved trees, or to no longer be able to make your way along the trail past the fallen trunks. Couldn't even get around them on the cliff sides.

The damage from this snowfall provided the fuel for the terrible fires which followed. The trails were blocked with fallen trees. The broken timber and branches were so thick, a person could not make their way very far.

It was still winter in New York. There had been no luck in finding a publisher, only rejection and hurt. Peter was very glad to hear from his friend, the back country patrolman, so he packed up his clothes and books for storage, glad to leave New York where he had failed again. He hated living in New York anyway.

Pamala, a good girl and dancer from California, was staying with him off and on. He was sorry to leave her, and their last night together was spent in bed by the large windows overlooking 104th Street and Riverside Drive, looking at the fine architecture of the houses there—gray stone and iron-work. It was quiet in the city for a little while, free of the sirens and running feet and shouts on the street and horns blowing. He lay there with Pamala and cried. She was a good girl, quiet, and expected little. She let him do what he wanted with her, always.

"I'm sorry to leave you," he said.

"I'll see you again." But they never came together again, and he lost track of her. Too many changes of address.

Peter drove those thousands of miles across the continent in his old car, excited that he had a job. When he arrived, he went to see the chief of the forest there.

"We don't have any work for you," he was told.

"What?"

"I don't know anything about a job."

"But Bill said that if I came out here, there would be a job waiting for me."

"Well, I'll call Bill and see what he said."

"Yeah, I told him we could use him," Bill told his boss. "It's my fault."

He was hired and assigned to trail maintenance, but only after he had an expensive physical which they made him pay for. He was sent out to the ranch where his ranger friend lived. The main office rented him a post office box out in the country within fifteen miles of the remote area where he was to be stationed. His mind was filled with visions of horses, mules, chain saws, long stretches of trail and deep forest and stream crossings.

But by the time Peter arrived, there was bad news. "Well, my God, Peter, how the hell are you?" They talked awhile, no more than a minute, and then it came— "Well, Peter, I lost you. They radioed ahead. You've got to leave here now and drive over the mountains now and report to work on the Coast at eight in the morning."

"What?"

"That's right. You ain't stayin' here. They took you away from me. Said to get you over there now."

"For how long?"

"I don't know," he said. "But I bet they're goin' to try to drive you out."

Peter was badly hurt by this. He had come all the way from New York to work with Bill. They both were upset by it. Bill wouldn't work with just anyone.

Peter was too tired to leave then. It was about a three hour drive over a treacherous dirt road, to the Coast. He waited until the following morning at the crack of dawn and drove over the mountains.

Peter's memory of the ranger's cabin was strong in his mind—with its wooden walls and kerosene lamps and bantam roosters. There was a stream in front of the place, and the sound of it was sweet. The water was sweet, too. Large spreading California oaks shaded the place, and lots of fruit trees. There was no electricity or telephone at the ranch, but Bill had a two way radio, propane stove and a refrigerator, and Coleman lanterns. The hens deposited one or two eggs in the same place on the porch every two days, exactly in front of the door. That way they kept bill out of their coop.

It would have been fine to spend the summer there.

Peter reported to work and was put on a road project. He was bitter about the assignment. The road had been rebuilt each year for three or four years and had been substantially redone three times that year alone. "They ain't sealing it properly," a local resident said. "It's deliberate. You know, *make work!*"

For long periods of time there was nothing to do until a truckload of oil came. The men stood around breathing in asphalt. Inactivity in the hot sun made Peter uncomfortable. The boys he worked with flagged traffic and kept people away from their homes and from trucking their children to and from school. The faces of the locals were sad. But there was no reason to keep them out, as no work was done.

The oil truck came. It was the wrong oil, and had to be returned, delaying the project another day. There was no excuse for such an error, but typical of deliberately screwing things up to run up the bill. Men were kept idle that much longer. If someone wished to inflate the budget with cost over-runs, incompetent mistakes were the way to do it. If an engineer was trying to maintain his empire against being phased out, any delay might buy time until a change in policy would save him.

On the third day, Peter was told to spread asphalt. He looked at the black, hot, bad smelling stuff and looked at his new fifty dollar boots, new uniform pants and shirt—back country clothes.

"Take this shovel and spread that stuff," the chief engineer told him. He was one of those California pave-its. California was being paved over, and he had come down especially to tell Peter what to do. The boss was lean and tall, with a square face. His green trousers and khaki shirt were finely pressed, his face closely shaved, his hair neatly trimmed, cut short in the style of another age. The engineer's motto was *pave it*. He was brought up in the tradition of California's *pave it over*.

He had come all the way from Santa Barbara to sadistically torture this greenhorn and see if he could get into his ass.

Peter stared at the asphalt, and the spot on the dusty road where it was to go. Two long minutes passed. He began to say something, but hesitated. He was frozen with an acute anxiety block. The engineer must have thought Peter was a very strange bird and some kind of a trouble maker.

"Take this shovel and spread the stuff there," the man repeated. Peter's vision began to restrict. The anxiety block gripped him and would not let go. He didn't belong there. He could not go on smelling that terrible stuff. They must have known he was an asthmatic. They must have seen his military records about that. After all, they were the government, and they wanted to get rid of him. He wanted to walk off the job. He was sure a hell of a long way from Harvard, fallen from grace once more. He felt tight in the chest and could not breathe. The asthma tore at him, asthma that he'd concealed during the physical. He could not breathe.

"I'm sorry, but this is not why I came here."

"Come out to this road?"

"No. From the East."

"Where did you come from?"

"New York."

"Jewish, are you?"

"No."

"I thought everybody from New York was Jewish."

"Not at all."

"Well, I know they have a lot of Spics there."

"There's people from all over the world."

"Yes, I know about that, come to think of it."

"It's very cosmopolitan."

"That's the trouble. Why did you come here?"

"To work in the forest, in the interior, doing trail maintenance with Bill."

"I didn't hear you. What were you going to do here?"

"Back country work. Clear trail."

"Well, hell, son! Ain't nobody been back there from the Forest Service in years! Least ways, in most places."

"Yeah, there's a ranger that works back there sometimes. Bill. Clears trail. They've got to keep the way open to Cone Peak, you know."

"Well, we're goin' to let all them trails go. I don't care if they take them all off the map. Throw all them hippies out of there. We killed some of the sons of bitches back there, growin' pot and stuff. Burned them right out! Don't want any trails to make it too easy for them to hide out in the back country. That was quite a raid, by the way, with sheriff's deputies and the Highway Patrol!"

"I drove all the way from the East to work back there."

"Well, you're here now. You've got to do this if you want to work."

"No. My job description says trail maintenance. I don't have the clothes for this. I saw the way the boy's boots were ruined by asphalt and oil. These boots of mine are brand new."

"Mister, we're here to pave roads. As far as I'm concerned we ought to let the rest of those trails up there grow over and keep the Goddamn hippies out. We come to work prepared to work, with our work clothes on. You go on into town and get yourself some new boots and jeans."

"I didn't travel so long a way to spread asphalt and work on roads. The stuff is dangerous to breathe. It's a dangerous substance. I didn't sign up to work with a dangerous substance."

Peter was unaware that the budget of that forest showed several hundred thousand dollars for trail maintenance. They did not actually spend any of that cash, because it was merely part of the Government's Black Budget, concealed in the padding for the innocent Forest Service, HEW, and such. Like the engineer said, they never cut a single blade of grass in the interior, but they got from him what they wanted: someone up front on the payroll doing trail maintenance. Meanwhile, the engineers had seized control of the Forest Service in those parts, and were milking it for all they could get.

Peter turned and walked up the dirt road to the highway. He was given one more opportunity to work and was sent to the Forest carpenter, and old and crotchety man of sixty-eight, to be his helper.

Peter's new nick-name was "Hey." The old man called him: "Hey, get me my crescent wrench!" A sixth sense led Peter to the right compartment in the truck, one of many, and the right tool kit. Fortunately, he knew what a crescent wrench was.

"Hey, get my ball *peen* hammer!" Again, the tool was found quickly. At least he could do something right.

"Hey," the carpenter ordered, "get me that small cold chisel.... Hey, get me my pipe wrench—the big one.... Hey, I want the Sedgewich saw."

Now, what the hell was that? "The what?"

"Sedgewich. Don't ya know nothin'?"

"Oh."

"No, no. That's the wrong one. Get the Sedgewich."

After four saws and angry grumbling from the carpenter, Peter accidently brought the right saw. "Hey, get me my monkey wrench!"

"Oh, okay."

"Heh, heh." The old man was starting to like Peter, after trying to wreck him. They worked hard and fast, and Peter got into the rhythm of the job for many days. He mixed mortar, shoveled sand and gravel, dug holes in rock and dirt for cement pads, put together forms and screwed screws, searched for the right size nut in a large box full of hundreds of nuts, swung a pick-ax, dug trenches and poured cement. He forgot about the incident on the road, and waited or hoped to be transferred back to his ranger friend Bill and do trail work in the back country.

"The way things are done here," Pete, the old man said, "is to build somethin' and then tear it down. Then ya build it again. Keep things goin' round! This is a damn Mickey Mouse outfit. See that generator down in the shed? They keep changin' it. We got that old World War II navy Waltzing Matilda that works fine, but they get one of these computerized generators in here, and the more complicated, the better, because it just runs up costs that much more and creates that much more work. The idea is to pad expenses. You know who's payin' for it!"

"The taxpayer."

"You get an 'A'."

Then Peter learned he was assigned to a fire fighting crew in another month. They figured he'd quit working for old Pete, but he didn't, so they had to try something else to get rid of him. They needed him on the payroll for trail maintenance, but now they wanted to drive him out. Or get him killed in a fire.

He liked the old man, crazy as he was, and the work was good for him, to try to get into some kind of shape again. He was out in the fresh air. But Peter wasn't ready for fire fighting. It was dangerous, and he couldn't run. Men were often killed during forest fires. His boss to be had two men killed the years before, so they transferred him. "They shouldn't have been there, and that was the boss' fault," it was said by many.

The old carpenter seemed angry and bitter much of the time. "This is a Mickey Mouse outfit," he would repeat, and grumbling about the silliness and absurdity of what he had to contend with. They all lived in a double-wide trailer—their barracks—and the carpenter disliked the piles of dirty dishes, muddy floor, and the mice the young boys left. Pete complained, and rules meant to keep the barracks clean were put up. The younger boys actively hated the grumpy old man.

The engineers figured Peter would quit when they put him to work with the old man. No one had ever been able to work with him before.

The carpenter would not let just anyone work with him, either. But Peter did not quit, and had taken a liking to Pete. He liked working with a competent man, not with someone incompetent or deliberately sloppy as the engineers were. Pete planned jobs, and no time was wasted. He didn't put up a front and dress neatly, either, because he didn't have anything to cover up. No matter how much they hoped he would make a mess and have to re-do something, he did it right the first time. So they just wrecked what he built, and started over.

There was a rhythm to the work and it was satisfying. Peter did not feel that it was stupid, senseless, or *make-work*. When they deprive a dissenter of meaningful work, no matter how lowly, they destroy him.

At times Peter was allowed to use the whole spread of tools and power tools: drills, Skill saws, table saws and so on, and at these times Peter could forget about wanting to work in the back country, as long as he could learn how to do new things. He liked everyone at the station. Pete would often cook a very fine dinner for him, at the end of a hard day of labor, and occasionally made pancakes for breakfast, and prepared lunches. In this way, Pete won Peter's loyalty.

Peter discovered that he was the first person to be able to work with the old man in a long time. They would have to stop that! After work they often went to the café a mile away and had beer. Peter came to know that the carpenter accepted and liked him, and had no realization that Peter was educated or honored in his own way. Had Pete known the true nature of Peter's background, they might never have been able to work together.

The old man changed and became garrulous and kind to the other boys and within two weeks his relations with others seemed transformed. The close quarters of barracks' life shifted from hostility and bickering to one of warmth, comedy, community, and mutual pleasure. The boys saw the good side of the old man and overlooked his grouchiness. They even began to clean the barracks and wash their dishes regularly, and pretty soon Pete was cooking for them too, and offering them a glass of wine from his stock of cheap, good, California red.

It was good clean work out there in the ocean air, but evil forces were at work. Many top men—station foremen, fire-fighters, patrolmen and others had transferred out. There was a cancer in the organization. A new replacement came up from down south near San Diego where there were right-wing armies, units of the American Nazi Party, and other militant or non-humanitarian persons who did not like the United Nations. The new man announced himself: "My family is from Germany and I believe in the iron fist."

"Well then," Pete said, "We might as well start right here. I believe in the iron fist myself, and I've got one, if that's the rules you want!" Pete wound up as if to hit him, and the New Order cowered in his chair, afraid. The Old Order—Pete the carpenter—was as tough as nails, his strength undiminished by the years, and no doubt would have destroyed our punk with one blow, driving him into the ground.

A long list of new rules went up in the barracks, including one that threatened inspection of personal gear at any time.

The boys, who'd been working very hard, said, "I don't know if I can take this!" The new station foreman, who'd been briefed by his boss, an ex-deputy sheriff who was asked to leave by the town he worked in because he threw his weight around. The boss made our arrogant new Nazi feel as though he was the leader of everyone, when he was only a fire-truck driver, with other slight responsibilities. He began to give orders to the geologists and recreation manager who lived there. The geologist lived in the only house at the station, with his wife and baby—a fine new place. The new foreman bunked in the barracks with the boys, which was a terrible situation. The recreation manager and the geologist were fine people, and unknown to anyone, the geologist was a friend of and close to the Forest Supervisor. One of the college boys working at the station was a friend of the Forest Supervisor, also, so the lines were drawn between the good guys and the red necks.

There was a power struggle between two groups. An entrenched band of civil servants—men who could not be fired—were pushing every one out.

Good guys are here defined as men who try to get along without hurting others, try to make things work, are humble and not arrogant, and who are sensitive to others. The bad crowd treated and spoke of the boys as 'muscle' and not people. Men were killed in fires because bosses held these attitudes, and ordering the men to take shortcuts down the wall of a canyon against the rules, down a "chimney" towards a fire.

The Chief Engineer was one of these people. He bulldozed down fence posts when they might have easily been salvaged. He used four-inch pipe when two-inch pipe was enough, and the cost of a four-inch gate valve would buy all the easily used plastic pipe the station could use. A leech field for sewage was constructed that could accommodate twenty times any possible amount of sewage the station might produce, and this ate up the maximum amount of funds, disguised under the Solid Waste Disposal Act, as well as chewing up a large piece of landscape.

Engineering projects proliferated down near the Coast Highway, while the fragile, brilliant trails far back in the mountains, built at such cost, overgrew. Trails that had been built by the CCC by hand with pick and shovel during the Great Depression, trails that were a great joy for men and women to walk and hike—four hundred miles of them in that forest alone that no vehicle could traverse, leading through the mighty redwoods and great mountains. Trails that would be sorely needed and lost when the great fires came not so long after.

"I hear the mountain speak," the Indian said. Peter listened to the trees and the stream, and was moved by their spirit.

"Pave it," the Los Angeles and Santa Barbara people said. The quiet and peaceful trailer park at the Station, surrounded by owls on top of the light poles at dusk, and haunted by coyotes and lions at night, was torn up. Bulldozers and graders were brought in, outside contractors paid, and paid under the table, and they paid back under the table, where merely some weed cutting and flower planting would have done the job. The bulldozers came for weeks and shifted the dirt around in the trailer park, while the public spilled out of the hot cities, and could find no quiet place to park their cars and campers, for all the camp sites were filled. The people spilled out of the blistering cities and parked along the highway for want of a better place. They made camp fires in illegal and uncleared places which often set forest fires.

Some poor families might have been bused to the forest, if there were facilities, to ease their daily grinding poverty, to come close to nature, to the sea, to God, but the money was spent on a large trailer park that would never be used. There were only three trailers there. There would never be more.

Every single engineering project was blundered by these blockheads, and money wasted.

Rage boiled within Peter from a lifetime of injustice. He was studying, reading, researching. He would find a way to go for the throat of the terrible corruption of life at every turn. He would find a way to expose their worst crime. Their worst murder. He was quite mad at times.

Then one day the Chief Engineer came. They were all having lunch in the office. The Chief Engineer suddenly addressed Peter. "What do you think of John Kennedy's policies?"

"That's a strange question to ask!"

"I understand you are quite an authority on his murder. You say there was some kind of conspiracy or something. That Oswald didn't shoot him all by himself, is that right?"

"Oswald didn't shoot him at all."

"No? I heard he did. I recollect the Warren Committee said Oswald did it. Wasn't Oswald some kind of a Communist?"

"I don't think he was a Communist, but I don't believe that he shot the President."

"Well, then, who did?"

"It was a domestic plot, a conspiracy. A *coup d'état*."

"But from where? Where did it come from? The Mafia? Name names."

"No." Peter did not want to answer, and was acutely uncomfortable. The room was deadly silent. What the hell were they talking to him about this for? Where did they find out?

"The CIA?" the engineer asked.

"Maybe."

"But why did they kill him? Was he a Russian spy or something?"

"He was going to be re-elected."

"Maybe he was too liberal. What did you think of his policies in the Middle East? Wasn't he pretty strong for Israel? Maybe it was them that killed him, after all?!"

"Yes."

"Well, then, we have to have that oil. Why shouldn't we be friendly with the Arabs?"

"Maybe."

"Didn't you tell someone he was killed by the War Party?"

"He had started the withdrawal from Vietnam. They didn't want that. They wanted to go to war."

"But, who is *they*?" He said it mockingly, like all those who ridiculed the idea of any conspiracy. Anyone who doesn't believe in conspiracies is nuts. "We have to fight the reds and Commie sympathizers."

Like me, Peter thought. "Here, you have a copy of the April, 1975 *True Magazine* right here. I'll read something to you," Peter said. He picked up the magazine and read. "This is from Victor Marchetti, the author of *The CIA and the Cult of Intelligence*: 'The more I have learned, the more concerned I have become that the government was involved in the assassination of President Kennedy....'"

"So? Who is Victor who ever he is? So he's some guy who writes books. So what? Does that mean he knows anything? He's not the government."

"He worked for the CIA."

"Well, I'm not going to believe some traitor that violates his security oath."

While Peter read, he realized who the informant was, that it was a man who lived a half mile away, that had been in contact with someone back East about Peter. Peter had talked with the man a number of times. He had been present when John Kennedy was killed in Dallas taking photographs. He was a journalist.

The country had become one vast conspiracy of silence. For some, they did not dare talk about the assassination.

Peter had gone to Dallas that December just after Kennedy was killed there. He had gone back several more times, asking questions, interviewing a few people. Little did he know what a big role he would play years later. That he would conduct a major investigation of his own.

The engineer had leaned over and read the writer's name off the article. "Well, who the hell is Marchetti?"

"He was an executive at the CIA."

"What funds are you being paid out of?" The Chief Engineer suddenly asked Peter.

All the hands were present, except that the station manager was away, the #2 man was out sick, and the #1 man was down south. The time to strike and get rid of Peter was now, at hand. It happened with the next breath. Unexpected. But the man had to have his fun prodding and poking the victim before he squashed him.

"I don't know. I don't understand your bureaucracy."

"Well, I have no money for you. The only thing I can use you for is spreading asphalt. As far as I'm concerned, you're terminated."

"You mean, I'm fired?"

"Yes. I can't use you."

"What about Pete? Who's going to help him?"

"One of the boys here will help him."

"I hate working with Pete," one of the boys said.

"Well, that's it. I don't need you. I can't use you. I've got to have muscle down there on the road project."

"I like working with Pete. Why can't you get someone else?"

"No. I can't have men picking and choosing what work they will or won't do. I heard all about you."

Sadly, Peter walked away, with some anger. He went to his quarters and packed up. The money he had ahead would not last very long, and he had not quite covered the cost of the trip West. He was tired from the hard physical labor and dispirited. Oddly, though, he felt free. Free from the Gestapo in the outfit. The boys had gone through the baggage of the new Station Chief that morning and found a suitcase full of Nazi paraphernalia. They planned to do their best to take him out and get him smoking dope and sucking off some little boy and compromise him. They had it all planned.

"You had them frightened," the geologist said when he returned. Peter camped nearby, waiting several days for his check to come. "They made a serious error when they hired you. A smart man on the bottom, doing nigger work, can see everything that's wrong. You can see what the inspector or the public can't see looking in from the outside. They are afraid of you. Real afraid. Especially of a writer."

As he drove away he thought that there was no end to it. That he would be driven mad. But he didn't think they might try to kill him.

He stopped at the store up the road nearby for gas. The man who lived near the station, whom he believed was in touch with people back East about him, was getting gas. He had been present when John Kennedy was killed.

"You know, you have an obsession," he told Peter. "You ought to forget about it before it's too late."

Coming back there, to that same forest, as he now had done, would nearly cost him his life. But where else could he go, and he wanted to live outdoors for awhile. He was tired of abandoned houses and dirt cellars in the city when he was not working at unloading boxcars or cleaning dye tanks.

"America is the very incarnation of doom. She will drag the whole world down to the bottomless pit," wrote Henry Miller.

Chapter 4

▼

Time passed.

He camped nearby, sometimes in the camp grounds on the cliffs over the ocean, and sometimes inland a few miles, shielded by the Coast Ridge, and looked for other work when going to town. Peter wrote letters and called long distance to the East, to try to get things straightened out. Nothing worked. The time camping was good for him, and helped mend his tattered soul. He read, researched, and wrote a little. He needed rest but the food he fed his brain with rested his being and he gained strength. There had been too many shattering experiences.

Peter had to face a part of him that wanted to die, wanted to commit suicide, and on that spot by the San Antonio River, he realized that he either had to kill himself, or stop thinking about it. He had lived with it long enough.

His unemployment insurance finally came through, and he would be secure for a few weeks as long as he could live outdoors. There wasn't enough to rent a place. He bought time, and mended. But it was sure cold there in the mornings and late at night.

He spent the time in exile reading, and learned everything he could about the assassination of President Kennedy. What did it matter and why study such a thing?

What they did to the President was a symbol of what they were doing to the country. To the world. To him. To get along, go along. Don't rock the boat.

You either accept illegal contracts given out by a corporation, or don't do business. Die. You accept the way things are....

Peter knew and understood things about the assassination that no one else knew, and at the time the principal researchers were far off the track. One could say that the leaders had co-opted the citizen's investigation for the purpose of bum-steering everyone away from any suspicion that all of the evidence in the case was manufactured. Who had the power and ability to do that? What group of conspirators? Peter did not realize that once he pushed his way in with the group that had co-opted the issue, he was marked even more than he had been. They would get him if no one else could. Their task was to make targets out of nosy people and the innocent.

He made a connection and was sent to Dallas by an alternative news organization. A lawyer for one of the Dallas policemen told Peter that Jack Ruby did not come down the ramp into the basement of the police station to shoot Lee Harvey Oswald, but Ruby had came down in an elevator with the assistant chief of police, Charles Batchelor. Batchelor had been in charge of security precautions for the motorcade in which President Kennedy was shot, and was in charge of security precautions for Oswald. He later became the Chief of Police. That was his reward.

President Kennedy had fired the top command of the CIA for betraying him at the Bay of Pigs. The Deputy Director of the CIA whom he fired, was General Charles Cabell. Cabell was directly in charge of the invasion. His brother was the mayor of Dallas.

Cabell had sabotaged the operation because he and the Director of the CIA, Allen Dulles, had failed to trap Kennedy into following up with an invasion by American forces, an invasion that could only fail. Kennedy figured out how they had tried to manipulate him, and he fired them. They hated him for it. Hated him enough to help kill him.

Peter had seen the autopsy photographs of the President.

There were a few sets around, which were known as the "Family Jewels." The so called *Family* was much like an organized crime family, though those who had the pictures and said this deluding themselves with altruistic claptrap and did not realize what they were saying with their Freudian slip.

The official government photograph of the back of the "President's" head was fake.

Peter knew it and could prove it, he thought.

It was night, cool along the edge of the ocean, and there was a strong wind blowing. The Coast Highway clung to the edge of the cliffs and the waves crashed on the rocks far below. Peter drove along—avoiding the rocks that fell to the road from the cliffs in the night—thinking of the dark redwood canyons to his right, wondering when he would be able to go hiking again, wondering how long the forest might wait, before a fire or developers took it away.

The developers wanted Big Sur. They wanted it badly. The Forest Service stood in their way on part of the coast, so the developers had to subvert the Forest Service from within. "It's not right that the Federal Government owns so much land right in the middle of California," some people said. They wanted to pave it, or build on it. Privatize it.

His car had been having strange things go wrong. The brakes failed one day, and a mechanic in Berkeley—where he went every two weeks to get his unemployment check—took five hours to find the problem. That ate up a large part of his check. Almost all of it.

Finally, after paying for new brake shoes he did not need, they found the problem. A small brass fitting which held the shoe in place had one of its prongs broken off. Maybe it was sawn off. It sure looked like it was sawn off, and the mechanic offered that opinion.

Peter had camped in a Forest Service campground after being fired, and from time to time he saw some of the men he'd worked with the year before. One of them convinced him that his carburetor needed overhauling. Peter let him work on it. He did not trust this man. He knew they wanted him out of the area. The man had killed before and told the stories to Peter. He'd done it for his country under orders.

Peter thought he smelled gasoline from the time he began to drive north along the remote coastline from Pacific Valley. The odor was quite strong. He had been driving ten minutes or so, and the smell was disturbing. He came to a bridge repair project on the dark highway. It was cold and windy, and there was no traffic. The temporary stoplight at the bridge was red. He braked the car, and noticed that the generator lamp on the dashboard lighted, as he pressed the brake pedal. Strange, Peter thought. Some kind of a short.

"One by one they die under the most mysterious circumstances—'suicides,' auto 'accidents,' and 'apparent' heart attacks. Can it all be extraordinary coincidence, or is it part of a sinister plot to liquidate the people who hold the key to the murder that still nags at the world's conscience," *Saga* headlined an article by Penn Jones, once, in 1968.

Not that Peter didn't see it coming. He knew that the man in the Forest Service who had worked on his car was retired from the military, and had worked with the CIA from time to time. And the DIA. Most of all, he worked with the Office of Naval Intelligence. The area was swarming with agents. They had to protect the electronic battlefield and the new laser weapons technology being tested at Hunter Liggett Military Reservation.

The gasoline smell became much stronger as he waited for the light to change. Peter got out of the car, leaving the engine running, and went around and opened the engine compartment in the rear, shining a flashlight on the motor. The wind whipped his thin shirt.

Gasoline poured all over the engine, as it idled. He dashed to the ignition key and switched it off, and the engine stopped, making a long silence in the deserted place. Peter waited two minutes or so until the gasoline evaporated and the engine seemed cooler to the touch. He had driven about five miles or so, for ten minutes. He realized that they had meant to scare or kill him. He wasn't far enough away. They were probably on the road now, with the truck. They would have hit his little Volkswagen from behind, the way they did to Karen Silkwood. And kill him.

He had to get out of there fast. They would be coming.

The engine had come close to catching fire and exploding. The only thing that saved him was the coldness of the night, and the wind, blowing the gasoline away. The engine had got quite warm, but not warm enough yet. The wind blew the vapors away.

He saw that his headlights were on and quickly put them out. Then he spotted a hidden turnoff up ahead past the bridge behind some bushes. He quickly started the car and drove it off the road and hid it from view. Then he ran to the engine while it was still running, watching it for a moment in the light of his flashlight. Gasoline rippled over the engine in large amounts from all the seams in the carburetor, and poured from the new plastic tube carrying fuel into the carburetor. He ran and turned it off again.

The Forest Service man had replaced his fuel line with a length of plastic surgical tube. The tube was loose and nearly slipping off the carburetor. He examined the twisted bits of wire at each end of the tube meant to hold it tight. The ends of the wires were twisted together in a spiral. The wire at the top of the tube had only one end twisted around the other, which remained straight, so that the wire was not tight around the tube, holding it to the carburetor, and the tube was almost off. The wire could not possibly hold anything. The wire had to be braided but it wasn't.

They had tried to blow him up and failed. He kept a sharp eye on the road. A few cars came by, and a couple of trucks, but he did not get a good look at them.

Then it came. He could barely make out the green Forest Service fire truck rolling along in the dim light. It would have been quick. The truck would have rammed Peter's little VW from behind and pushed him over the cliff to the sea in a fiery explosion.

But they didn't spot him and the green truck evaporated into the darkness.

He got the old fuel line and replaced the plastic tube. He then tested the screws holding the carburetor together. There were about fifteen of them and every one was very loose and required at least three complete turns to tighten them.

He waited about an hour after making these repairs in the gathering darkness, and then drove off, thinking it not wise to stay there too long. He drove without lights, feeling his way along the road in the darkness. He could see a long way ahead, and behind him in the mirror, but no more cars came. The silent rocky walls of the mountains close by rose from the road with the spectral shadows of trees looming forbidden, massive, thousands of feet above him in a great wall against the ocean and his own insignificance.

Each time Peter braked the car on curves, he noticed the generator lamp come on ever so little, on the dash, indicating that there was a short somewhere and that the electrical system was discharging. A spark might have exploded the gas. Soon the battery would be dead. He had to get to town.

When Peter came to Monterey, after a two hour drive, he was quite tired. He stopped to buy gasoline and asked the attendant to watch his tail lights to see if they lit when the brakes were on.

"Do they work?"

"No."

"Are you sure?"

"Yes." His tail lights not operating, Peter had been set up for a police traffic stop.

He had a frosted glass of draft beer at Bossos, his favorite tavern, on Lighthouse Avenue in New Monterey. The bar was ordinary, but he had gone there for years and had always liked it.

He thought that they'd get him sooner or later. Somehow he would go on trying to beat them. To win. But win what? It did not occur to him that it was a no-win. The important thing was to *fight*! Right or wrong, he could not go up against the power of government or industry alone.... He was non-violent, so how could he fight?

Sometimes he knew he was crazy. He was possessed. Compelled. But he was a writer and that was the only way to fight: with his pen.

The only way to resist, for him, was to go for the throat. For the jugular. Expose the worst crime they had committed: the assassination of President Kennedy. He hoped that might earn him some clout.

Fat chance!

Later he discovered that the fuel nozzle inside the carburetor had come undone, and that the brake lines on the master cylinder were crossed and shorted so that he had no brake lights, and might have been hit from the rear. His engine was in the rear.

Chapter 5

▼

Peter thought it was best to take a powder for awhile, and get away from the violence. He drove 300 miles north to Mendocino and Fort Bragg, and sometimes as far as Arcata and Eureka, but stayed in Caspar in a decrepit, crummy, two-story wooden structure with cheap rooms over a bar for ten bucks a week. He'd long ago given up trying to live in Berkeley or San Francisco. But perhaps the anonymity of the city would have been better. He just wasn't any good at surviving there. Well, maybe. Peter had done it before with temporary jobs. For now, he wanted to be closer to Nature.

Peter had gone from the frying pan into the fire. "The land is evil up there, in Mendocino and Humboldt. Lots of drugs. There are evil spirits in the mountains up north," Hosanna said. Bob "Bear" Greenwood was potentially dangerous and threatening. A big, tall, burly man, he ran drugs that had been unloaded from ships that had come from South America off shore onto a Fort Bragg fish boat. They gave away drugs on the street in the local towns when a shipment arrived, and paid off the sheriffs.

The wheels of one truck that had backed out onto a dock broke through the planks and was stuck long enough for the cops to nab them. Bear's territory reached to Pacific Grove and Big Sur, and he supplied a café on the main drag of P.G. that was a central distribution point in that old Methodist sanctuary for blue haired ladies summering in tents beneath the cypress and sugar pines.

After making his drop, Bear drove the thirty miles to Big Sur and laid back, making his final deals. But sometimes he went on as far as San Louis Obispo and Morrow Bay, rather than staying put and make himself a target. But that was more extra driving.

Peter was acutely nervous around this crowd or anywhere near them, and avoided the whole deal. The drug gang knew Peter was too straight, and didn't like him. They made each other nervous and were afraid of troublemakers of any kind—wanting to keep a low profile. They agreed with Peter's take on November 22, 1963, but just a few years after those events, it was still too hot for anyone to open their mouths. Peter was a magnet, attracting trouble.

The Senator wrote by return mail: "I appreciate your recent letter advising me that you sent me information concerning Jack Ruby and the Tippet murder. I have checked my files carefully, and I find no record of having received this material. I very much appreciate your interest, and I would welcome an opportunity to examine your evidence if you have a second copy which you could forward to my office.

"Again, thank you for your interest, and I look forward to hearing from you." The signature was in ink, and it was the real thing.

The Chief Justice, Earl Warren, had ordered that all critics of the Warren Report be surveilled. This was translated by the FBI and others to "destabilize." To deprive of civil rights for some.

What did it mean for an ordinary citizen to stick his nose into such things? Suppose they knew something that was of value? Did anyone really want the truth to come out?

"When I was a Rabbi in Berlin under the Hitler regime, I learned many things. The most important was—that under such tragic circumstances—bigotry and hatred are not the most urgent problem. The most urgent, the most disgraceful, the most shameful.... is silence."

Peter went to the Post Office in the town along the Pacific where he had moved. He tried to talk to them. "I haven't received some letters here...."

"Did you put in a change of address?"

"Of course. Twice. Do you see this letter?" Peter showed the postmaster a letter. "It says that they sent documents to me weeks ago, to this address. And this letter, from a friend, here, saying they wrote to me, here."

"Well, you don't know that they actually sent the letter," the postmaster said. "I can assure you that there are no irregularities in this postoffice."

"Look at this letter I sent to a friend of mine back East. It's postmarked *Dallas* on the back of the envelope. Why was it routed through Dallas cross country, and post-marked there? Is the government trying to tell me something?" Like, Dallas took over the United States?! Is that the new Capital? The Associated Press did the same thing with the JFK case. Stories emanating from remote parts of the U.S. were routed through their Dallas headquarters and censored or often killed.

"That sometimes happens."

"Look at this letter," he said, whipping out some more, "and this one. This says they sent my royalty statement to me last October first at Columbia, then it says the company sent the statement to me here, a duplicate. I never received either one." Peter remembered stories about that post office, as he stood there talking with the postmaster, saying that they opened a lot of mail there. The Red Squad in Sonoma and Mendocino Counties were super active. They went after anybody that looked out of the ordinary, such as people trying to start publishing companies, as Peter was trying to do. *They* had to know about people seeking to influence public opinion, like teachers, writers, reporters, and publishers, didn't they?

Like the way they smashed the Morning Star Ranch in Sonoma. But then, those people were just barefoot hippies and dope smokers sucking off welfare.

"We've made a real effort to help you. We wrote these people to try to trace your mail. We even made a copy of their replies for you."

"I'm sorry, but I don't understand you. *I* made the copies of those letters, at my expense."

"You seem to be implying that we are taking your mail. You've said that in the town."

"I don't think I put it that way. It's obvious that considerable mail is missing. Does it have something to do with my assisting Senator Schweiker's investigation of the murder of President Kennedy?"

"The postal inspectors came all the way here. They made an effort. They have five counties to cover. Five and one half counties. The case is closed."

"The problems are continuing. What about this one? This is a registered letter to the United States Senate. Here is the Senator's letter saying he never got my letter, which was registered. How could a registered letter disappear? Here is my receipt for having sent it. I have never received the return receipt. It was just swallowed up. Disappeared. Vanished."

"It happened on that end."

"What happened to it?"

"*They* must have a reason, if they are opening your mail."

"What? Who is *they*?"

"Whoever it is!" The postmaster had slipped, had blurted it out. They were opening his mail, and the postmaster knew it.

"You don't know?" He was on the edge of hysteria. He saw in a flash that as soon as he walked out of there, the postmaster would be on the phone telling his superiors in Santa Rosa that Peter was not going to dry up and blow away. The idea, then, was to get him to move along and get out of there.

"You did not put changes of address in when you left New York or Berkeley."

Peter's voice rose. "Is that what the postal inspectors told you? That's a lie! A lie! I put them in the day I left. In duplicate. In triplicate. I'm not stupid. They just threw my mail away. My friends picked up mail for months from the lobby of the place where I lived. Off the floor. Out of the rain." He paused. A cold shudder ran down his spine, as he remembered that mailmen were found with bags of mail in their rooms, mail bags found in attics, mail found in the woods. He had thought—not quite expressed in his mind—that far more was going on than he could see. There was a pattern. He recalled reading *The First Circle* by Solzhenitsyn. Recalled all those stories from Kafka. Had he not read *The Trial* and a few other books, Peter would have lost his mind. *The Trial*, even the film, "Three Days of the Condor" gave him a bench mark that suggested what he was experiencing was not unique and had a reason. Such things described in the stories of other victims really did happen.

"I'm going to the FBI tomorrow. I'll take a lie detector test." He didn't know that they didn't work either, and that they could be rigged. He thought that the mere willingness to take the lie detector test would demonstrate his innocence. But what was he accused of? Of being radical? What were the secret accusations against him that were destroying his life?

"Go ahead. Do whatever you like. You aren't going to tell me how to run this post office."

"I wasn't!"

Furious, Peter walked out of the post office not feeling—somewhere between boiling and stunned. He was far away from things in the East, where he might be able to straighten things out. He would have to go back three thousand miles and try to set things right. But he knew he would fail. He never could get it straightened out. It would simply have to die of old age, like him. Dry up and blow away. Or, as they say, time might heal wounds.

To get along, go along. Play ball, or be closed out in the cold.

Peter had tried to set up a small publishing business and had found a printer. His printer was threatened. A person who worked there, whose agent was in the East—the same agent who had stolen some books from Peter right out of a publishing house—said to the printer, "If you print that book, I'll wreck the presses."

Many bad things started to happen to him in the town, as soon as he tried to get off the ground and publish books himself.

Hope still lived in him. He was afraid of hope dying.

That was why he had escaped to the West and tried to start over again. Dreams came true in the West, before it became a military province. He had created a publishing company, and that was one of his dreams. Years later after long periods of being moribund, of being sheltered and nurtured through lean times, it would come along and save him.

But his paper company had no office, no capital, and no distribution for his product. He had many ideas of how to make it work, but it was on a shoestring and doomed. Try as he might to raise money, to get someone interested in it, anybody with half a brain could see that the venture would lose money.

Should he, an artist, be trying to engage in business? He was going to try, and learned a lot. He learned book production from top to bottom—a valuable skill.

His first project in the attempt to break out of his shackles was to reprint his first published novel, but he couldn't get it distributed. He listed a post office box in the book for an address, but the post office was afraid of fraud and did not like that. He was a person with no official credit rating or record of being in business.

It had taken a great effort to get his little company off the ground, but all it did was fly low. Very low. His paper company kept flying for a long time, however, so low not too many people saw. Thirty years. Some other small presses were around that long but barely able to compete for a share of the market.

"You will have to use a false name," the dean at Harvard had told him. He'd said that several years before, when the trouble started.

On the street, a dark and sinister character, tall, with a heavy black beard, sunglasses, a black hat with a broad brim and round crown, a black jacket and darkened jeans came towards a fifteen year old walking alone on the street. The desperado pulled a small brown pill bottle from his pocket and offered it to her. He held it out in the open for over a minute, walking along with her. She stopped. Money passed. The bottle changed hands. This sinister character worked in the local medical center for a doctor who took cocaine every other day. A doctor who had been thrown out of practice in the city for writing too many of the wrong prescriptions.

One county Peter lived in was so corrupt that everybody from the sheriff to the judge and the county commissioner was on the take from the drug people. The local government would not tolerate outsiders, and hid behind a facade Baptist of fundamentalism and self righteous patter. They came down hard on strangers like Peter, and a many good people were sent away to jail to cover for the crimes of others.

Peter caught a glimpse of the ocean at the end of the street. Giant combers came in from the sea, as wide as the river mouth, sweeping in majestically and fast. Tall and cresting. They broke on the rocks and cliffs in huge blasts of glistening spray fifty feet into the air. Sometimes the breaking waves flung their foam, white in the sunlight, much higher, above the cliffs themselves. That was the only purity in this life, he thought. Pristine nature. And they wanted to bulldoze it away, cover it up, and pave it over. The pave-its would destroy all that lived and moved.

Bear came up the street, someone he barely knew. Peter had to talk to someone. No one there was really his friend. He had not been in the town but a few months. He was angry. The words spilled out. "I've had it, Bob. Have you had trouble with your mail, here, ever?"

"Many people have."

"Have *you* had trouble with your mail?"

"Yes."

"I just can't believe it! I thought mail was sacred. I can't imagine someone taking my mail. I've had it. I tried to do something fine. I tried to start a company that might bring capital and prestige to this town. Something cultural to California, which, God knows, it needs. The West needs this kind of thing. Now look at it! They are smashing up what I tried to do."

There seemed a conspiracy of silence in Mendocino. He noticed a few people at the Hotel from time to time that looked like laid back hit-men. Talking to it confirmed the suspicion when a man evidently needed someone to talk to and told him that he was just back from a killing. The town was a "cooling out" location. The whole area was heavy into drugs, and the fish boats came in with cargos from Columbia and Mexico late at night, landing on the beach, or coming right up to a dock in the inlet from the sea. Some of the bigger ships hove to off the coast, several miles out, and contraband was run in by small boats at night. Flashlight signals pulsed along the beaches and from headlands in the darkness.

One truck was so heavily loaded out on the end of a dock that the wheels broke through the planks, and it was forever stuck. Those idiots were caught.

There were isolated airstrips in the area, where small and large planes came in, fast Cessna's, old DC-6s, and even older DC-3s. Convairs. Anything that could take a short landing strip.

That stretch of coast had been unspoiled, untouched, and it had come under the protection of the Coastal Commission. But the Mob sent their spearheads in to soften it up. First came the dope. Lots of it, spread out among the young people—many of them just fourteen or fifteen. When a boat came in, they handed cocaine out the next day to buy silence and friends. Two-legged mules were needed to help unload the boats and stash the stuff in a hundred temporary hiding places.

Shortly after one of the boat loads of coke and grass arrived, a large old truck towing a heavily loaded trailer came all the way across the country from Maine. An antique dealer had bought up all the old buggies and wagons he could find, dissembled and packed his truck and trailer with them. He parked on the main drag of Mendocino and after a sandwich and coffee, began unloading his buggies on the street and assembling them. Word spread quickly into the countryside to farms and ranches, and as fast as he got a buggy set up, men gathered around with thick wads of cash in their hands and dickered on the price. The buggies were bought up fast and he sold every single one—more than thirty old time carriages, buggies and a couple of buckboards. Soon horses arrived and people went about the town driving their buggies in fine style, smiling and tipping their Stetsons at the ladies.

The Mob wanted the houses and land which belonged to the low income Portuguese fishermen and their families. They got them to sell when the price was right, and when they wouldn't sell, they raped their pubescent daughters, corrupted their sons, terrorized their children, sank their boats, and burned a few houses. They made the area so unpalatable that it wasn't worth it to stay there. Houses that had only been worth $5000 suddenly went for $95,000. Money flowed in the sewers.

They brought in dozens of laid back rock bands who regrouped there, and who acted as a drug distribution network throughout the U.S. The particular beats and rhythms promoted along with the drugs, created an iron-clad political control over the nation's youth, just as drumming is used among primitive tribes to control their energies.

"Some of those religious sects that stay away from popular music know very well what they are doing," Peter wrote to a friend.

Soon the Holiday Inns and Taco Villas, Jack-In-the Boxes, Burger Kings and MacDonalds would eat up the landscape and perch on the cliffs over the ocean. Soon the Coastal Commission and the environmentalists would be defeated inch by loophole by inch. the fragile ecology along the edge of the Pacific would be destroyed.

Bulldozers were lined up, engines running, wheel to wheel, tread to tread, ready to carpet bomb the land running down to the sea, just as they had done to Cannery Row, Cambria, Santa Cruz, and a thousand other lovely towns in California, the Golden Land. Packaged fisherman's wharves were waiting, ready to roll out of a tin over the water, complete with stand-up tourists and prefabricated Irish and English pubs. Keep things moving around, and capital turning over. Get everybody visiting everywhere else and you pyramided the money on deposit in a thousand banks, while the industrial base was destroyed. And you destroyed what was for what will be, imposing uniformity and conformity on the land.

Every so often, the land got them all back, and moved. Big time. Mother Earth didn't want to hear it out there. The land quaked and rolled, upthrust and slipped sideways or dropped down. Terrific thunder crashed, and that would be the end of their piss dreams. Mother Nature was becoming angrier and angrier at the U.S. and the world.

Beside, there wasn't enough water, anyway.

Peter saw the bookstore proprietor—an older, smiling Jewish fellow named Mordechai. Mordechai seemed real nice and it didn't occur to Peter that the guy was an agent of change or of somebody else. His smile was perpetually pasted on: "From that paranoia known to Jews—fear of rejection, of the master race," he had once explained to Peter. Peter was headed into the local restaurant.

"Come in and sit with me," he offered the book seller.
"I never go in there."
"Why not?"
"I don't feel welcome."
"Come in with me today, will you?"
"No. Come down to the shop if you want to talk. This is a small town," he said. "I am all alone here. Far away from my people. It's like one group against another. One gang of thieves against another!" he said, laughing.

Consuming and devouring, lacking the anonymity of the city, where people could disappear into the crowd.

Chapter 6

▼

They sat on a rock in the forest, talking. He needed to talk. He hadn't known the young lady long.

"Just once," she said, "I wish they would tell us the truth."

He listened to an animal in the forest, moving slowly through the trees, step by step on the leaves, until the big beast was out in the open, in a clearing. He stood for awhile in the middle of an acre of open land, its large head and antlers dominating the air around, listening, majestic, silent. After a time the moose moved on, very slowly, fearlessly, the King of the land, across the clearing until it disappeared into the trees again, on the other side.

Then someone took a shot at it.

A long way off they could hear the river rushing in the canyon below.

"I am so tired," he said.

"You must be in danger."

"Yes. I think so. I'm never sure."

"Why did they kill him? Kill Kennedy?"

"You know what I think? I think it was because he was getting laid. He was attractive to women. I often thought that was at the bottom of it. Nixon never slept with his wife the whole time he was in the White House. He got out of touch with the smell of reality and that's what went wrong with him, I bet. The bad old men that own and run the country couldn't stand it because Kennedy was attractive to women. Why, the director of personnel at the CIA, a Mormon, sat in judgement of that poor gal who came out for the Equal Rights Amendment for women, and he ex-communicated her!"

"Why did they really kill President Kennedy?"

"I see I can't get a laugh out of you!" *Let me see your titties*, he thought. *Let me put my hands on them.* Like Charles Bukowsky, he would write anything for her, tell her anything she wanted to know, if she would do that for him. That is, if it was true. But, he told her anyway.

"Tell me."

"He had started the withdrawal from Vietnam. They didn't want that. They always heat up a war in an election year, and he was trying to stop one."

"And that's why they killed him?"

"Yes. It was the War Party. They wanted the war in Vietnam. They need wars. Wars make money. They don't intend to win them. They stir them up wherever they can, until someone reacts, in Afghanistan, in Africa, somewhere. Nations need diversions, like carnival sideshows. It's a form of entertainment. We tried to outdo the Reds. John Kennedy said that 'we cannot, as a free nation, compete with our adversaries in tactics of terror, assassination, false promises, counterfeit mobs and crisis.' It was that kind of thinking that got him killed."

"He was too liberal!" she said, taking a deep breath.

"Yes. But they used the Puritans to justify killing him. Those who sit in judgement of the rest of us. Never mind what they themselves do that's wrong…"

"Do you think it will ever be exposed?"

"I think we're moving towards some sort of new investigation."

"When?"

"Soon. There are bills in Congress about it now."

They were quiet for a moment. They could hear the silence of the forest and the stream far away.

A look of horror spread across his face. Peter stopped talking, remembering. After awhile, and cried for a moment, quietly. He drank with John

Kennedy once. He remembered that voice, the laughter, the warmth of the man and his handshake. His mind.

He saw that tragedy related to his own. Those in the middle, the center of opinion, were being squeezed, silenced. He had been in the center, he thought. But he knew too much. Too many trips to Dallas.

"I am so tired," he said again. He did not know how to get started again with his own life. Brute labor was killing his spirit. If there were labor camps, and if the dissenters were simply put into them, then maybe there would be some moral support from the other inmates, but this was crazy. He was so alone.

His grand obsession with the assassination was destroying him at the same time that it was his salvation.

Peter couldn't keep his mouth shut. He had taken a strong stand against illegal practices in certain industries. It was like a union v. management dispute, except that he was all alone. They made sure he did not get a good job, and they made him crazy, like someone berserk, until he acted that way, and built up a bad record. It was just like Russia or any other totalitarian state. They isolate the victim and let him roast until he or she dies in agony.

He was being run to ground like a scared rabbit.

Chapter 7

▼

No one knows. No one knows.

A long way off he could hear the river rushing in the canyon below, like far away surf, running, like the wind in the great redwoods.

A hummingbird came by, flitting here and there among the leaves, feeding on an iris for a moment, then on some poppies and lupine.

Peter began to feel threatened with violence in the town where he had gone to find peace and quiet. He felt watched, and of course he was, as any stranger in a small town would be. It was not subtle.

The postal inspector drove up one day from Santa Rosa without notice, while he was away. They always operated that way. They did not send a card or call. They just came. Even if it meant a two hundred mile round trip for nothing. The inspector caused enough trouble, though. When Peter returned from a hike, he was told in tones of displeasure: "The FBI was here looking for you!"

"They asked a lot of questions about you."

"What you been into?"

"We didn't tell them anything. We said we didn't know you."

"They wanted to know if you were a chronic complainer."

"What did you do?"

"You been in jail?"

"The FBI? Are you sure?"

"Yep."

But after awhile, Peter found one person who had asked the man for his identification. Strange that people will talk to any suit who looks official, without asking who they are. "He showed me his card, and he was a postal inspector."

"What did he ask?"

"He wanted to know if you were a mental case. We told him that was probably true."

"Well, I've never denied that!" he said as a joke. Trouble was, his informant believed it. "What did he say he wanted me for?"

"He didn't."

"It must have been over my missing mail. I wrote them a letter bitching about that."

"Hey, everybody around here is missing mail. They throw it in the sea."

But Peter's reputation, such as it was, was destroyed in the town. Actually, since there were so many criminals hiding out or engaged in drug operations in Mendocino County, some might have been impressed, except that nobody wanted the heat around.

Peter went to the inn four miles from town where he lived. It was a place that rented rooms over a bar. It would have been a nice, atmospheric place for a writer to hide out, had there not been so much cocaine and heroin around. People that were into heavy drugs were very paranoid. He stopped in the bar downstairs for a beer.

The area was a rest stop for rock stars, mobsters and hit men. They even had their own doctors, and were serviced by specialists in drug and sex needs.

"The FBI was here looking for you."

"That was a postal inspector."

"Same thing. What did you do? Take somebody's mail? He said he'd be back. I don't want that kind of trouble here. I want you out of here by tomorrow."

"I'm telling you that it was a postal inspector. I'm missing some mail, and that is all they came here for, to talk to me about that. Look, I'm writing well in this place and don't want to leave...."

"You have to move out. It's too much heat."

"Heat?"

"Heat."

A man came early the following morning, just after breakfast, and knocked on the door of his humble room. He was clean shaven and looked like one of those Mormon Mister Cleans they stamp out at Brigham Young University in Provo. Maybe there was something to the "Mormon Conspiracy!" Peter would have to take another look at the *Gemstone Papers* and see if they covered that one.

"Are you Peter Casey?" he must have seen a photograph of Casey and had it memorized.

"Right. You are the postal inspector?"

"Can you come out to the car and talk? We can do it better there." The man was probably sick to death of tacky rooms in run down buildings, fearing he would smell dirty underwear, stinking socks and old tennis shoes.

"Can I see some identification?"

"Oh, yes, sorry. Here. My name is George Benson. I'm with the Inspectors Office of the United States Post Office."

They went out to his car and sat for an hour in full view of the bunch of bandits that lived there. Peter could imagine what the man thought of him with a lousy address like that. Peter hadn't given enough thought to the people that saturated Caspar. It was not a good place to stay. Maybe for them it was fine.

The lovely woman he had just begun to spend some nights with saw them sitting there in a green unmarked obviously government car, on her way to work. He saw her lovely body and remembered the week before when they had gone down to the cliffs over the ocean on a windy and cold night, and lay down on his coat on some ice plants and necked. It did not occur to him that she was on ice from some mobster or dope runner somewhere, that they had her stashed away, chilling out, working as a waitress at the Hotel. His taking up with her would antagonize an unseen enemy that had sat waiting, biding his time until *he* could get the girl, having her staked out as his territory alone. He would have friends, and they would all hate Peter for touching her. They would know about it, too.

She had taken him home with her to her house near the sea and taken off her clothes to get into an expensive red velvet robe that excited him enormously. And then they had made love many times in the next three days or so. And of course he told her many things about himself, and spoke indiscreetly concerning the President's death. "The Mob was involved," he told her. "And the government. Some people in the CIA."

"How do you know that?"

"I worked for a Congressman once. I was privy to a lot of things. An aide to President Johnson, Marvin Watson, told the FBI that the President had told him he believed the CIA killed President Kennedy." President Johnson deliberately directed attention away from himself, and the CIA was the Fall Guy!

"That's heavy." This was when Peter was still an amateur, just starting to dig deeper into the case, and he swallowed hook, line, and sinker the second levels of cover-up. Johnson wanted some people to believe the CIA did it, just in case a conspiracy turned up and Oswald didn't do it alone, so that he had something to direct attention away from himself. Johnson didn't want anyone to think *he* killed Kennedy.

She might have been from the CIA, for all Peter knew. There was something odd about her, and certainly Mendocino County was populated with people cooling out after government missions, including killings. She seemed to be somebody else, hiding, as though she knew a lot more than she let on, and had a major experience she had to get away from. Like him. Like them all. He became convinced that she was the girl in the polka dot dress present when Robert Kennedy was killed.

Often, after opening his mouth, he found that the people he was talking to had a father who worked for the CIA, or a mother who had worked for the FBI and didn't let on. Why should they tell him? Their children took an interest in him, especially, when he criticized those agencies. You never know who you are talking to. Their fathers thought nothing of running their daughters as agents. Often enough the children (like father, like son) took up spying on people as naturally as taking their morning poop, then ran and gave it to their dad. Spying seemed almost genetic or learned at home, but was passed on from generation to generation like families of cops or firemen.

Intimacy—a piece of ass, a sexual encounter—was the best way to pump someone for information. He was a lousy liar, lousy at keeping secrets, and he could be had. He was a first class sucker.

The agencies—the FBI, the CIA, even the DIA, didn't assassinate President Kennedy, but men in those agencies played a rôle. Men with Texas accents, and men in the Dallas Police Department planted the evidence framing Lee Harvey Oswald for the murder. The cops were promptly killed before December, 1963, was out.

Peter sat in the government car for an hour, and the whole Coast could see it or knew about it. "What letter is missing?" the postal inspector asked him. Mr. Clean squeezed a hand exerciser with a heavy spring between the handles, channeling off the desire to kill this worthless bearded hippie. "In a business like this, with so many millions of pieces of mail, things are bound to get lost." That was new, and a good cover: being a business. The Post Office department had been privatized within the government. It was true.

"You mean the *Post Office*?"

"Yes. In any corporation, especially since the Post Office was made a business by the latest reorganization, we make mistakes."

"Oh."

"Yes."

"But you work for the government?"

"Yes, I guess you could say that."

The agent took Peter's measure. He held him semi-prisoner in his car for an hour, studying him, trying to read him, preparing in his mind what he would write for the file about this seedy character who must have another self: the criminal self. All people were potentially criminals, or hiding their true nature, the G-man thought. Peter had longish hair. He must be a drug dealer!

"In a way, yes."

"You are trained with the FBI agents in shooting and so on?"

"Yes. I was on a stakeout last week, or I would have been here sooner to talk to you. Now, what letter are you missing?" He squeezed the hand exerciser with a series of fast, forceful movements, suppressing his impatience.

Peter had a file in front of him, labeled "Post Office," Patiently he explained what was missing, or what he thought was gone. "I never, never had a letter missing in my life—never had trouble with my mail before I became involved in this investigation."

"What investigation?"

Like a fool, Peter did not smell danger. He—being trained to answer questions in school, which was perhaps the primary function of our schools—naturally answered any question put to him.

"The murder of President Kennedy."

"I didn't know there was any. Didn't the Warren Commission close that case?"

"No."

"What are you doing in this 'investigation?'" Here Peter sat, in the government green car, in a remote area, in front of a remote country inn where he lived with a bunch of bandits over a bar, controlled by a drug ring that he knew nothing about, telling a government agent that he was involved in an investigation of the murder of the President.

Undoubtedly the agent knew all about the drug gang right there all around them, and thought that Peter must be somehow connected or getting connected or he wouldn't be there, and thinking that Peter must have been using the Kennedy case as a mask for criminal activities. There were a lot of self righteous criminals, in his experience, who pointed the finger at everyone but themselves.

Peter better start thinking about bailing out of that town soon. That's what they wanted him to do: Stay on the run.

"I sent a registered letter to Senator Schweiker, and he never got the letter. Here is his letter to me saying that he did not get it. I didn't get the return receipt, either."

"That does happen. But you see, look here, we investigated in Washington, and here is a copy of the list of registered pieces received at the Senate on that day, and the Post Office did deliver your piece to the Senate. Here is the number on the list, which is the same as the number on the receipt. So it got to the Senate. What happened to it after the Post Office delivered it there, I don't know. But we delivered it there. You have to recall that there are a lot of people working in a Senator's office and it is very unlikely that your letters would ever be seen by the Senator. Staffers are there to screen out the trash and make everything look nice."

"But here is the letter from the Senator, signed by him. It says: '.... I have checked my files carefully, and I find no record of having received this material....'"

"How do you know that is his signature?"

"Well, here is his signature on the envelope, and I have other signatures from him."

"They use a machine to write and sign those letters. Perhaps they threw away your material...."

"I don't believe that!"

"Oh. Did you retain a copy of the evidence you sent him?"

"Yes."

"May I see it?"

"Yes, but I don't have it here."

"Did you mail it?"

"Yes."

"From where?"

"I went down to San Francisco and sent it." Then he realized that might be an affront to the postal inspector, as Peter did not trust the Post Office there to handle the piece.

The question came, quietly, subtly, a little later in their talk, when Peter imagined his nuts, his skull, his fingers being squeezed to the point of excruciating pain in that heavy spring hand exerciser. "What was the evidence you sent? I was always interested in that case. It is fascinating, isn't it? What could you possibly find or add to the case?"

Peter knew that he was at the point of no return. That he had passed it and had joined that amorphous group out there that loosely linked, constituted an unorganized underground of lonely fighters, seeking to find and expose the truth. He knew that he could hide nothing, could not hide himself anywhere in the world. They had a dossier on him, he knew that, and sitting there with the postal inspector, he knew that there was no turning back, and that he would have to fight like the very devil or be destroyed. He might be destroyed anyway, but at least he would have fought to expose the truth, to overturn the illegal practices in the industry. Like the dissents of Oliver Wendell Holmes, who often stood alone, his dissent might become the law—might reveal the truth.

But he knew he was a fool. He had to just keep trying.

Peter could go to the remotest area of the country in what remained of the great rural outback of America, and not hide, that they would find him or find a way to make him surface, take his mail or deny him his rights to smoke him out in the open where they would work on him and threaten him. They would find him just as this man did, and would appear without notice to question or even harass him. He was shortly to find out what they would do to him on a new job because of this visit, to drive him out of work and places to stay, places to live. He would be driven from city to city, town to town, coast to coast until he could run no more. He would go mad if it continued.

"Anyone who knows anything about the Kennedy case is being watched. This phone is not safe. Call me back on another number now," His professor said over the long distance phone a few months before, not long after they had nearly blown up his car with him in it. He was given another number and called back shortly. It seemed silly, but he did as he was told. "Sorry to be so vague, but this letter might be opened by someone else," the professor had written. He had been one of JFK's teachers at Harvard, and was trying to get Peter to more seriously investigate the case.

There had been a *coup d'état* in America.

Peter did not tell the postal inspector anything more. He tried to be as nice as he could. But for the first time in his mind and life, the authorities began to be the enemy. He had never feared police before, and had always been patriotic. He had not mistrusted his country, had not understood how it lied to everyone, to itself.

How it maintained control.

Not long after, a lawyer told him, "If you keep sticking your nose into this stuff, you can expect to be killed!"

Peter moved to Arcata, another town some miles to the north, farther from the city. Very far. He was trying to stay close to nature as long as possible, trying to gain strength from the outdoors, from the sea and from the mountains and the forest.

And, he was a survivalist. He thought that if it came to it, he could hunt and fish to stay alive, even without experience. Pick berries and eat miner's lettuce. Yes, he was getting crazier and crazier!

He missed the girl in the red robe. Missed her a lot.

Longing for a woman's arms and lying together naked.

Not long after moving to Eureka, a large registered envelope came. "This package has been opened," the post master told Peter, and he named a post office where he thought it might have happened. "Please write that on the face of the package," Peter asked him, "that it had been opened."

The post master wrote "Received 9/10/75. Plastic tape over original postmark! (signed, Supt.)" And indeed, there was a wide piece of tape over all the postmarks. It was his entire legal file, sent from another lawyer. Perhaps very valuable for *them* to read!

Peter sent the envelope to the postal inspectors, at the request of the post master, who did not want to get stuck with the crime. They returned it to him, saying that the piece "does not reveal evidence of tampering or opening." Sure.

At a bar one day having a beer, a man from the last town where he'd stayed—a dope ring man—moved in on him, moved up close. "Stand back. Give me some room." But the man moved close again, his malevolent eyes glued to Peter's.

"Stay away from me," Peter told him, pointing a finger at him.

"That finger is going to get you in trouble some day," the man said, and grabbed his finger and bent it backwards, almost breaking it.

Often, Peter stayed in his room alone reading a great deal. He read the testimony of the doctors at Parkland Hospital where John Kennedy died.

Dr. Paul Peters said, "We saw the wound of entry in the throat and noted the large occipital wound." There would come a time very soon when Peter would go and talk to those doctors, and Dr. Peters would write him.

None of the doctors had ever seen the autopsy photographs. Why not? Why did the government withhold the pictures from them? They would have instantly declared the pictures fake, and not of Kennedy's head and body. Or at the least, that they had been altered.

So would have the widow, Jacqueline Kennedy, who held his head in her arms in the car. She knew they were fake, and later got that message to Peter. That would have blown the case completely apart, but almost at the moment he was to interview her with a video camera, she was dead. Jackie had caught galloping leukemia—the kind that only comes from having her apartment seeded with uranium pellets, which is what happened to Karen Silkwood who worked at Kerr-McGhee in Oklahoma, when she got too nosy, though she was actually killed in an auto accident on the way to meet a reporter.

Before he died, Jack Ruby claimed that he was being injected with cancer cells. How would he know about that unless he was privy to the project in New Orleans, which he was, that was creating an injectable cancer bio-weapon to kill Fidel Castro?

Peter explored the deep woods away from the coast and electricity some miles into the back country, and visited or stayed with people and other rustics that lived there, getting along with Coleman lanterns and wood burning stoves and kitchen ranges. It was rough, but they felt that they had escaped a regular life, the tax man, and those who would persecute them for smoking dope. It was a very hard form of existence out of the previous century. They chopped a lot of wood, and the hands and fingers of the women were no longer lovely, if they ever had been.

He bought a Coleman stove for one mountain woman in heavy boots and a granny skirt with two children, but could not get along with her. Other people took his gift the wrong way. So she returned it. She was afraid he or somebody would own her if she kept it. He was normally generous if he had it to give. Eventually his generosity would come back and bite him when he was foolish with what he had. Some lessons in life come hard and too late. Some people can give it all away.

He explored the chances of working as a wood cutter or dishwasher in a logging camp, but that work was tied up solid. It would take years living there to get on to something.

A lot of hard years to make any kind of a life at all in that remote part of America. It was like the backwoods of Maine or Québec. And logging would die out, the big saw mills close. The last mill in Fort Bragg would finally close, and the stinking bad air would blow away at last.

Maybe it was a good thing.

Chapter 8

Peter finally got a job teaching a course of writing at a local junior college. The college was very conservative. They were so conservative they barely paid for that one course. But he was glad to be teaching again. Glad to be doing something.

He had met the chairman of the department in a bar in Mendocino, and the man liked him and asked him to come down for a visit, then hired him part time.

When he had come to teach the course and was interviewed for the job, they put him in a room with the entire English Department, and he was questioned ruthlessly for an hour or more by these small timers, with all the petty pedantry of narrowly focused minds locked into the mental gymnastics of their particular out-patient encounter-therapy group. Their professional jargon was a hybrid argot of the United English Department, pop psychology, and a mental ward.

That is, they had at him with ravenous appetites for his soul, thirsting for blood, his mind, his feeling, like vultures—like all the critics in the world trained to pick like carrion the brains of their enemy: a *writer*, a *real* writer, and get some of his strength. The real game was to try to destroy him on the spot if they could, or at least put him in his place.

In the end, nobody in any English department had the slightest understanding of how it was that someone could write, of the enormous powers of concentration and memory necessary, and so they—like most—tried to consume and destroy a real live writer, examining him beneath a magnifying glass like some squirming insect. Peter was a caged animal in that room, muted, already doing battle with titans who someday would direct their stooges to march him right up to the wall where they would shoot him.

"Are you a good teacher?"

"Yes."

He showed them his credentials. His recommendation from Harvard read: "...He brought to his classes an energy and devotion which were remarkable. His passionate commitment to his craft, his frank and unpretentious manner, and genuine affection for people gained him the loyalty of many students. He does not fit into any of the usual academic or professional categories. He is an independent, original, and strong-minded man. I was very glad to have known him." See, even then, he was a trouble maker.

Peter had lost none of his fire in spite of being dragged through the gutter. But a person has to fit somewhere. Where the hell was he going to fit?

Peter Casey better find a place soon, or die.

So they paid him $45 a week before taxes, and camping out at first, or staying with friends, he got by. Then he stayed in a dormitory for part of the summer when he was asked to teach a second course (four months was not long enough to utterly wreck him).

When the political evaluators came from the state, they passed out a form to the class, asking them to grade Peter. He got an almost unanimous "A." But the evaluators found fault with him nonetheless. They said that they saw no teaching going on!

Of course, he worked with students privately in his office, and did not allow them to criticize each other's work in the class. Their egos were too fragile at that age, he believed. That wasn't what they were paying him for. This method of teaching went against the herd.

He let his students organize the class. He wasn't there, in his opinion, to train teachers and scholars and critics, but he was there to help them with their writing. He read only their best pieces. Criticism was not allowed. They were free to do that on their own time, but he discouraged negative criticism of their work among the students on their own time. He tried to protect them from each other and the viciousness young writers practiced among themselves in their colossal egos. He trusted only himself to crit their work.

This was a deadly error. Writing courses were subtly used to impose the discipline of the United English Department—as laid down by IBM and the "Iowa School" of writing on otherwise free spirits.

His mind was shattered by the past several years and he was so filled with fear that his emotions were on the surface. At the same time that Peter was teaching, he desperately tried to get the FBI, the ACLU, the U.S. Attorney—anyone—to look into his case. He was barred from publishing. He knew that the contracts the industry used were illegal, and that they would do anything to silence him. But that really wasn't what caused his nightmare. It was a symbol of the arrogance that allowed an abuse of power, and that was what did him in. The abuse of power is what does most of us in when we are targeted by the arrogant. We do it to ourselves, too.

This kind of thing would eventually push anyone into a life of crime as a means of staying alive. That was the idea: to get him into trouble. He would do it to himself unless he was very strong.

"Please help me," he wrote at the bottom of every letter. What a sap!

One night, shortly after beginning to teach, he saw an FBI man waiting a few feet outside the door of his classroom. The man, whom Peter had talked to a few days before, was still there when the class was over. This shook him up.

He was under surveillance. Why?

Teaching at that community college was a bit like teaching at Harvard again, except that the students were mostly older, married, and veterans. Some of them had a great deal of talent, and they could tell a story. They talked politics often, and the philosophy of education. He tried to avoid politics, but there was no way to do it, since the students insisted on it. It led to trouble.

As at Harvard, he never had more than one person absent. Of course, he was required to take attendance, and like school children, the grizzled

Vietnam war veterans and mothers of children dutifully came to class and sat in their little seats with a folding wood surface just large enough to hold a notebook to make notes on. They could put their bundles, lunches and books in the compartment underneath their ass in that brilliantly designed self contained unit.

There was a succulent, juicy eighteen-year-old girl in the class with lovely breasts who regularly drove him crazy. But she was glued to her boyfriend. The way she looked at him, though, and knew her power over him…He dreamt about her and the way she wet her lips with her tongue when she saw him look at her tits or in her eyes.

His class talked about the CIA and the Tri-Lateral Commission ruling the world. These people might have been in the great rural outback of America, or what was left of it, but they wanted to *know*. "*Just once*," they said, all across the nation, "I'd like to be told the truth." From your students, though, you will learn. His students often amazed him with what was in their heads and the large amount of information they had, in such a remote outpost of civilization as that God forsaken barbaric village.

"The CIA is not an intelligence operation, primarily, Peter said. "It is for clandestine operations. That is why the Directors: Richard Helms, Allen Dulles and so on, are always from Operations. That's why we never know when the next Pearl Harbor is going to happen to us, and it is always such a surprise when some other countries start to fight or invade somebody because of what the CIA's operations department has been doing there—and we aren't told about that."

So the state sent in their evaluators week after week and the blue haired little old Republican ladies from the school's hierarchy came and sat in the back of the classroom. "I hope you don't mind my being here!" they said. But the class did. He couldn't teach right, either, under that kind of scrutiny. The evaluators came down from Sacramento, sent by Ronald Reagan's boys, and they watched him, and the FBI stood outside the door. It turned out that the FBI agent was a close friend of Mr. Clean, the Postal Inspector.

Peter Casey was obviously a security risk, if not a foreign agent.

And they wrote him up. They twisted and distorted things. They picked apart his language and quoted him using the current California slang, which his entire class depended upon every minute of every day.

"Far out," he said.

"*Really!*"

"I was into that!" he said. They took note after note, writing it all down, and surely the room was wired somewhere. They listed his phrases and language. When he used the word "folks," it went into his record. They didn't like that word. The Language Police in Paris and Québec City had nothing on those people!

The Chairman of the English Department—not only there, but at another college where he later gave a lecture—whispered, "Don't talk in here. My office is wired. I think they've got my phone tapped. Watch—when we come out of here, he'll be standing outside the door reading the clippings on the bulletin board, or he'll just happen to be in the next room, or just happen to walk up to me the moment I put the phone down. We are all being watched. This is a police state!"

"Who is doing this?"

"Dean Roberts. He's the Dean of Humanities here. You see...." He said, "I asked a lot of questions about the assassinations too. I didn't tell you that. They think I'm a radical," the Chairman said. "None of us are safe here. We can lose our jobs in a heartbeat."

"Well, thanks for hiring me. I hope I didn't get you into trouble."

"I figured you would talk too much, but the students are too important and it was worth taking the chance to have them exposed to you. It's just one course. You'll have to think about going somewhere else next semester."

"I'm not having any luck. I doubt if anyone will hire me."

"Sorry."

"This place kind of reminds me of a high school gym. It's like high school, not like a college."

"You have that right. It isn't Harvard or Yale. They are just as controlled, too, in their own way, as are the community colleges run by local governments."

"Some of the veterans trouble me. One of them has a degree from Stanford, yet he is working on an Associates in Arts here."

"The new push in the education industry, in this business, is to get your second degree," he paused, a sad look on his face. "It's just a business. Don't knock it. It provides work for a few more teachers. Maybe he can keep collecting VA benefits that way. He was in Vietnam. He earned it."

"You know who I'm talking about?"

"Yes. He was in ONI—the Office of Naval Intelligence."

"Yeah, well, I think he's surveilling me for the government."

"They all will. It's the nature of California since governor Ronald Reagan turned it into a police state. He made it a military province." There it was again. "Everybody rats on everyone else. It's from the *lettres caché* to this!"

He was asked to teach again, in the summer session, and they offered him a room in a dormitory. They did not have apartments for visiting faculty, and he would have a roommate. The set-up was fishy. He had been told that he would have a room alone, but they assigned him a roommate—a thug who had just been released from San Quentin. Peter did not want to appear unliberal, but the fellow scared the daylights out of him. Soon, the rules of The Joint seemed to be imposed on *his* life. The summer rapidly became a nightmare.

Incidents were manufactured, and Peter began to be afraid. Here he was, teaching a course in the school, and being subjected to a brutalizing dormitory life with a bunch of drunken jocks and living in tremendous noise and confusion. All the while, bottle blond plastic Barbie Dolls from La Jolla with no underwear threw themselves at him. Naturally, he couldn't resist one of them, although he knew it was *danger*.

But nothing came of it except a few quick orgasms on a nubile, pneumatic and brainless California blonde. It made him sick. Without love or feeling. She was being unfaithful to her boyfriend and trying to get a better grade.

His roommate grabbed Peter's arm one day, and threatened him, and Peter went to the boss and demanded another room, fast. He got it, but not right away. It was clear the ex-con had been pointed at him with a word in his ear from one of the authorities. All they had to say was "he's a child molester," and someone would take a shot at him or try to fuck him up without investigating.

Within one more day, serious trouble developed. They had him on the run and out of control.

The temperature was a 110 and 115 degrees for a week or more. His brain fried. The others were used to the heat, but it wasted Peter. Peter thrived on cold weather only. He liked winter.

He taught until ten o'clock at night. It was brutally hot when they left the air conditioned classroom, and still about 115 degrees. The heat struck him like a blow.

"Come on, lets go have a beer," one of the war veterans said. Some of the class went along. They went to a pizza parlor for food and beer. They had fun, and Peter drank two beers, talking to them about their writing and politics. Two of the married women with children where there, and they made one of their weekly propositions to him. They both wanted to take him to a motel and help him out, they said, jokingly. But these floozies would never come across. They were just kidding.

The women wrote about the pain they experienced in their marriages, and the husband of one beat her. It was a form of therapy for them to write about their lives. The woman who was beaten said she had only one outlet in life: to write. She was a terrible writer, but he didn't tell her. In fact, few of them were more than semi-literate, but even those that were not literate at all were groping to tell some extraordinary story that certainly, he thought, was worth telling, worth trying to help with. Everyone has a good story, and he believed he could help anyone get it out and make it read well. Peter was out to save the world, too.

Finally, after the others went home, there were only two students left, the Stanford graduate, and the CETA employee, both Vietnam war veterans. The Stanford vet had an intense look in his eyes, a glitter. His eyes were piercing, searching, hypnotic. Maybe he was on smack. He had worked for military intelligence.

"You ever hear of *Operation Desktop?*"

"No. What's that?"

"It's the implanting of intercontinental ballistic missiles on the ocean floor. That's what the *Glomar Explorer* was all about. Retrieving the sunken Soviet submarine was just a cover for the *Glomar*. In fact, some of those sunken subs never sank. they didn't even exist. They were just a cover for what was really going on!"

"Oh. Gee."

"I really like your class. I love the way you teach!"

"Thanks. But what the hell are you doing in a junior college?"

"Getting the G.I. Bill."

"They pay you to go to school? How can you get away with that? You have a degree."

"They pay me." They paid him because he was a spy on the other veterans. Both of them were. They were leaders of the Vietnam Veterans Against the War in the area, which was co-opted. They could cut anyone's funds off they didn't like. Their main job was to report on their fellows, but one of them did not know what he was doing. He too was drugged all the time, and was being used by the Stanford man, who was his control.

Nothing rang right.

About midnight, they left the bar, and the veteran drove off. Peter got in his car and went back to the dormitory. It was still blistering hot and he was sick from it. He was disturbed by the veterans and married women in his class. It all seemed so strange. There was an undercurrent of something odd.

Another of the vets, who had left earlier in the evening, wrote at length about serving in the National Guard during the Watts riots, about the trucks moving through the streets and encounters with the "niggers" there. He wrote with hatred and aggression at times, but the man wrote passionately and very well. Peter thought that his story should be expanded and that it might be a valuable historical record, in spite of the man's terrible prejudice and race hatred. Peter thought that maybe by befriending him, he could change the way the man thought, and lever him out of his hatred for others of a different color.

It was strange because the man was of Cuban origin and had been taught to hate blacks in this country. He himself thought that everybody should tolerate *him* and all Latinos, but not blacks.

They had chosen men from the countryside to go in and shoot the *niggers*, because neither were people to the other. *Niggers* were dehumanized and to be brutalized. It was easy once you had desensitized and programmed with TV violence National Guardsmen living on a white preserve in the country, like Polish Zomos kept apart from the population so they would have no problem beating and killing their own people if told to. Systematically, they were disciplined and bought and paid for, rewarded with veteran's benefits, perks and scams, easy money and hard times, carrot and stick, drugs and booze, new pick-up trucks and loose women. The whole area was loose, hanging loose.

As long as there was poon, food, wheels, beer, and a roof over their head, why worry?

"What are you doing teaching in a cow college like this? You're a high class guy, though you could use a barber."

"I don't know. I needed a little work, needed to keep my hand in." Then he told them a little of how badly things had been going, that he was black-listed. "If you make a man look bad enough, no one will care about him or want to do anything for him," he said.

"So what else is new? Don't be stupid! It was always like that."

"Why are you involved in this assassination thing?"

"I am against political violence. Assassination has become a political tool in this country, like Argentina and El Salvador. I think the public has a right to know that the government is just a front, that all these murders are conspiracies coming from the Power Control Group. That it's all a lie! Nothing has been right in this country since John Kennedy was murdered, and the government lied about it!" he said, from his soap box. But he had to give a straight answer.

"How do you *know* it was a conspiracy?"

"Because the back of the President's head was blown away, and they lied about it. Dr. Jones, who helped treat the President when he was dying, said that there was 'What appeared to be an exit wound in the posterior portion of the skull.' They faked the autopsy pictures to cover it up. Ten doctors and nurses testified to a large exit wound in the back of the head. That is what they are afraid to face, and will never face it. The Warren Commission lied about it!" He was speech making again, but it didn't occur to him. He did not see himself the way he was, at times. If he would just keep his mouth shut so they could give a clean report on him! But he thought he was Sir Thomas More.

"Kennedy was just stirring up the country," one of the vets said, draining his beer and signalling for another. "We have to have peace. That's the important thing. Peace."

"Oh...." *I don't know where I'm going, maybe straight to hell, but I'm going to cut a swath a mile wide getting there!* he thought.

"But wasn't the CIA taking the fall? Maybe the CIA was the patsy for the Joint Chiefs or Rockefeller, or the NSC, the NSA, the DIA or whoever was running things...."

They had all kinds of scams, those veterans. After a time, Peter found that several of his vets were handing in old pieces written for other classes that they had already been graded on. Some of them did not bother to even retype them. They were shaking down the government, but maybe they'd earned it in the crucible of Vietnam. That experience had built hate into the soul of so many of them.

Peter heard the stories of the slaughters, of the massacres of the old men and women, of young girls and children, of any young man who looked strong and healthy and threatening or even looked like a future threat. They did head counts, and paid for the severed heads brought in. They wore strings of ears on their belts, and sometimes scalps. Scalps of young girls. Whole towns like My Lai were wiped out by soldiers. That was just a drop in the bucket. The pilots carpet-bombed the countryside with B 52s, obliterating anything and anybody in the path of the bombs.

That was America in Vietnam. The truth, which the whole world knew except those who had been at home in America, was far uglier than any American would ever know or have to face. The world would make America pay for it. America would pay for not being able to control its government and her war machine. America would pay through the nose for her oil and her bananas and VCR's, for everything she needed, and they'd boycott American goods, because America was a rogue elephant in the world, without a head, without leadership. The public had lost control of their government, of its good sense and humanity since JFK died. The world was trying to tell America something. They hated and feared America. Americans didn't know it because this information was kept from them. They only heard about those who thought America was the greatest country in the world.

Peter drove up to the dormitory and parked in the darkness. He hesitated in the car for a moment, reluctant to enter his steaming room. The door of the car was slightly open, and a classical music station from San Francisco played over his radio. He did not want to go into the room with the man just out of San Quentin, whom they had not moved out yet. What kind of a deal is that, he thought? To give him such a roommate? Peter had tried, briefly, to relate to the felon, not rejecting him out of hand, looking for the good in him, but not after the man had grabbed him and threatened him. There was an undercurrent of violence that Peter could not live with.

He was listening to Mussorgsky's "Pictures At An Exhibition."

A car sped through the lot without headlights, and drove around madly in circles for some time, at high speed, and then suddenly came up behind Peter's car and stopped, so that he could not back out if he had wanted to. Then another car came up and hemmed him in from the driver's side, also without lights. They were old cars, without markings. No way to tell that they were police.

Peter heard a radio in one of the cars. Then he heard his license number over the radio, and realized they had radioed in his tag number to the police. He began to get angry. Sweat poured off him in the 115 degree heat. His brain broiled in its skull, totally unused to heat like that. It was very easy to go out of his head in the heat. Then a young punk came over to the door of the car and demanded to know what he was doing there. Just at that moment the headlights of the cars turned on brightly, blinding him, and the punk pushed the beam of a flashlight into his eyes.

"Lets see some identification," they demanded. How about their's?

"Get away from me," Peter yelled. He lost it. He had been driven too far in the past months to keep calm. "Get away from me!" he said. The heat had him in its grip, but there would be no forgiveness. He got out of his car and walked away. They followed him. He was lucky they didn't shoot him then. "*I teach here,*" he said. "*Leave me alone. I teach here.*"

"Stop. Police," one of them said. Peter didn't believe him. They had no uniforms, no police cars. They were undergraduates in a criminal justice program working as campus cops, and he was their victim. Punks. They followed him. He began running and running. And running. He decided not to go into the trap of his room, for fear of being beaten by the hoodlums.

The nature of Americans being what it is, the school had to cover it all up. They turned in reports and concocted all sorts of false charges. Since he didn't smoke dope, it wasn't easy to say that he was. What else could the punks get on him?

Long police reports were written out by the campus police about the "subject." He was their "subject" now, as were the subjects of the realm. The police viewed citizens as subjects. Here was a metaphor of the authoritarian state. From now on the incident would be known as "The Incident" and would be thrown up to him at every turn, as though he had caused them a lot of trouble, as though he was a trouble-maker and unworthy of the dignity and fair treatment normally accorded a human being.

The mess came to the attention of the administration of the college, which had concocted it in the first place, and of course, the town cops knew about it. He had something more on his record, something that made him look like a nut. One of those little incidents that would add up to someone trying to commit him as an unstable and violent nut. A trouble-maker.

He went to see the president of the college, but the man would not talk to him. "Get him out of here," he heard the president say to his secretary. Strangely, a similar frame-up had occurred three thousand miles from there the year before at another college where he spoke and was hanging out. They didn't want his political crap around.

Then he found that the school was cheating him on his pay. Short-changing political targets was a primary means of provoking them, of creating incidents.

"Why are you not paying me the full amount?" he asked the financial clerk.

They would not give him an answer then or for some time. No one seemed to know. But finally he found someone who knew what had happened. "You did not submit proof of your graduate degree."

"Why didn't you ask me for it?"

"I don't know," the girl in the payroll office said. "Ask the Vice President in Charge of Academic Affairs."

"The name of the game is rip-off, isn't it?" See, he wasn't handling this very well. Just stick to the facts.

"That's the way the school does things," she said. They were very literal.

"And all this time you figured I was a fraud? That I did not have that degree?"

"I heard something like that, yes."

"Well, I'll go get my degree now and show it to you," he said, and went to his room and got proof that he had a graduate degree. Eventually they paid what they owed him, but they didn't like coughing it up. It was too painful, evidently. They had not planned to tell him that they were cheating him. It was up to him to figure it out. That was another of Governor Reagan's tricks. Reagan who would become President.

There was a famous poster that was making the rounds in California then, before Reagan stepped on the backs of the downtrodden and became President of the United States:

NOTICE

MANY POSITIONS TO BE ELIMINATED BY MID-1967

In view of the 10% reduction of the budget, the California State Civil Service Commission will apply its RAPE pro-

gram to all branches of the State Government by midsummer of 1967, according to Governor Reagan. Particular emphasis of the program will be placed on the Transportation Branch. RAPE is the designation for the phase-out of many departments and stands for "Retire All Personnel Early."

Employees who are RAPED will have an opportunity to seek other employment. Those who decline to seek other employment will be able to request a review of their records before discharge. This phase of the cut-back is dubbed SCREW (Survey of Capabilities of Retired Early Workers).

One additional opportunity is promised by the Government for employees who have been RAPED or SCREWED. They may appear for a final review.... SHAFT. (Study by Higher Authority Following Termination.)

Governor Reagan explained that employees who are RAPED are allowed only one additional SCREWING but may request the SHAFT as many times as they desire.

A kinder, gentler America, we were not going to have just then.

Some of his mail was not getting to him at the college. The same old stuff. He began to watch the mail office in the dormitory and the girl in it a bit more closely, and one day he went to her, already knowing of certain letters to him which he had spotted at the main mail room in the administration building. She had put up the mail.

"Is there anything for me?"

"No." She seemed nervous.

"Don't you want to look?"

"Why are you bothering me? I know who you are, and I told you there is no mail for you."

"But, couldn't you take a look, please?"

"I told you there is no mail for you. Now, please go away and don't bother me." Was he on the faculty there, or what, and who the hell was she?

"You know, I teach here...."

"Yes, I know that. They never should have hired you!" What?

"What is that, there, on your desk?"

"Nothing."

"May I see it?"

"No."

He walked into her tiny office. "If you don't get out of here, I'll call the police! You're bothering me!"

Peter picked up several envelopes on the desk while the girl turned scarlet. She was shaking all over. All the envelopes were addressed to him. One of them was from the Central Intelligence Agency concerning his Freedom of Information Act request for his file.

Peter asked her to sign a statement that she had been withholding mail from him that day. "No!" she said vehemently. She was real mad, and close to tears at the same time. "Who put you up to this?" he asked her.

"No one."

"So, you just appointed yourself a spy and take my mail on your own, or are you nothing but a common thief?"

She said nothing. He tried again: "What are you going to do, save your country if you turn me in? Taking U.S. mail is a serious federal crime!"

Again she did not answer. He picked up her phone and called the vice-president of the school and told him to tell her to sign the statement.

"Read it to me," the man said over the phone. Peter read the statement he had scribbled out and the executive told the girl to sign it. She did. He got his mail, at least that day. A federal crime had been committed, but nothing would be done, of course. She was acting under orders of the government. This was political war!

Now and then he sent himself a test letter, and wrote something to put inside. Sometimes he just put ads from a magazine in them, or old letters. While teaching, some of these reached him. Some did not. Sometimes they would come marked: "This letter was inadvertently opened at the Post Office."

They didn't apologize. One day he wrote himself a scathing note that said: "To Whomever Opens This Letter: You are a traitor to your country. Anyone who opens anyone else's mail is not a gentleman and has betrayed their country. Leave me alone!"

Of course, this could be read two ways. It was. The mail lady at the administration building read it. Peter picked up his mail one day and found the letter slit open. "This was opened," he told her. "I accidentally opened it," she said. "I didn't mean to. I hate doing this!" It blurted out in the same tone as what she said just before that. She was an older woman, just past middle age. Vulnerable.

"Hate doing what?"

"Taking your mail. Why do you have to get it here? Can't you get it somewhere else?"

"Well, I don't live here. I'm just here for six weeks to teach the summer course. I was commuting 350 miles round trip here all last semester to teach. I have no other place to receive mail in the village. Beside, you take mail for all the other people in the dormitory."

"I know."

"Life is such that if things come together, then it's together, you know. Then it happens," one of his students said to him that night in a bar, when he was down in the dumps, with all that profundity of tone that only a Californian pontificating upon the vicissitudes and verities of life can muster. An eighteen year old country girl with an uncommonly luscious body and full and loosely covered breasts, talking, straining with all she had. A girl he would think about for many years and regretted that he couldn't get near her. She had a boyfriend and had been living with him since she was fourteen in a small hamlet some miles to the West of Santa Rosa, among the rolling hills of burnished wild oats and vineyards turned to Fall colors of unsurpassed beauty.

"Excellent!" she said, nodding her head sagely.

She activated the loneliness in his heart. Sometimes he drove out to the area where she lived, hoping he'd see her at the general store or somewhere. It didn't matter that she had air instead of brains, yet she could spout whatever she was required by the school, when her memory chip was fully activated. It didn't matter. She was kind. She was womanly. Erotic. Warm. Eighteen. She had already raised three kids for her dead mother, and played housewife to her father.

His students liked him, and they knew what the school was doing to him. They looked after their teacher as best as they were able, but they were old before their majority. They were already so beaten up by life that they seemed never to have had a childhood. They grew up too fast, starting at puberty. After all, they had their parents to look after!

Not that he might not have been drugged the night the campus cops set upon him. Set up, he was.

Her boyfriend came and got her and they drove away. Peter went alone to another bar and silently cried for a long time. The horror he knew in his heart from having his career smashed was insupportable.

He was just barely alive. He also wasn't alert to the fact that he was being followed from bar to bar and every move noted. Everything he said was being listened to. Everyone he spoke to was duly noted down.

As Peter headed for his room to go to bed, he was sure he saw a girl come out of it. She swung her hips at him and smiled in a lewd way. She was a Malaysian, and he remembered seeing her on the campus.

The day that his roommate, the fellow from San Quentin, had grabbed him, she had been in the room. The felon had swastikas tattooed on his body, and she had drawn circles around them with her nails. She picked up and examined things on Peter's desk, and brushed her body up against his. This night, she brushed her breasts up against him and laughed at him as she did it, then went away. She looked like she worked part time in a strip club. She walked that way, too.

The lock to his door was jammed. The lock took several minutes to undo.

He found the door open from the bathroom, which had been locked. Someone had entered from the adjoining room, going through the mutual bathroom. The fellow from the adjoining room was in the bathroom.

"How did this door get opened?" Peter asked.

"It must have blown open," he said, his voice shaking badly.

Well, it was a mistake to live in the dormitory in the first place. Other summer teachers stayed there. It was difficult to find a room cheap enough in the town to rent, on the salary from teaching just one course.

When he looked at the lock, he found that it was full of wax or soap, and that an impression had probably been taken for the purpose of making a key to enter his room.

His papers were disarranged on his desk. Someone had gone through them. He had no privacy at all there. No life at all. He had one chance to gain a foothold teaching and it had rapidly become a nightmare. It all turned to shit.

When he walked out of the room, a tall black basketball player jostled him and knocked him down. Peter went down on his knees. The boy moved on, saying nothing, apologizing for nothing. Evidently, Peter was just dirt.

"Hey, wait!"

"Fuck you, mother fucker!"

"Just a moment! What is your name?"

"What's it to you, *mother fucker*? **Fuck you!** Are you the police? Stick it up your ass! You know that girl you tried to get into trouble over your mail? I'm dicking that, get it? One more word out of you and I'll beat you to death." Then he kicked Peter in the groin. The youth was huge and powerfully built. Peter was beginning to get the picture. The boy's face was filled with rage and violence. He looked like one of the gargoyles on a French Gothic cathedral.

Maybe he was talked into the teaching job deliberately. They had him where they wanted him, and certainly made a target out of him. He was beginning to want to fly away, to flee, to give it up. But where could he go now? If he stayed any longer they would either kill him or he would die from what was going on....

Shaken, Peter went to his ancient VW beetle and drove off—going to another town nearby with a quiet bar where he might get his head on straight. He was beginning to hate the school, which was like the *Blackboard Jungle* on the college level. But then, this was for the poor. For the disadvantaged, and they were treated like children. To some extent it was an extension of high school.

As he started to drive, his car was nearly crashed by another. The driver was the fellow in the adjoining room to his, who shared his bathroom and everything else he had, who went with the Malaysian stripper.

They all went with her. She fucked anything that moved, as long as it was on a college campus. That was so she could give them what she caught on the streets.

Chapter 9

▼

The next day he drove down to Berkeley after receiving his mail, and as soon as he was on the freeway, a heavy one piece tank truck got behind him and began to tailgate him. The truck was a distinctive blue. He knew because he could not take his eyes off of it in the rear view mirror. The truck was so close he could see the rivets. He was trapped behind a car in front. Boxed in.

He was boxed into the left lane, with a car on his right. His little VW was pumping along as fast as it would go. He had the pedal floored at 65 miles per hour, but he was trapped, and could not get into the right lane. He couldn't pass the car on the right or slow down. The truck drew closer and closer.

Peter then began studying the shoulder on the left side of the road. There were bridge abutments every so often, and the shoulder would become non-existent. The blue truck moved to the right some, and straddled the divider between the lanes, tailgating the car alongside of him so that it began to pull over to the shoulder. The truck then began to pull alongside, very slowly, but half in the left lane, so that Peter and Old Stick, his car, was forced off the road onto the shoulder.

His heart was in his throat. He steered furiously, knowing he was one second from a terrible smash-up from which there would be no escape.

Suddenly Peter drove altogether onto the shoulder, seeing an abutment coming, and hit the brake long enough that the truck had to roll past him.

Then he pulled in directly behind the truck just in time not to crash into the bridge abutment, and tried to chase the truck to get the plate number. But the truck had picked up speed to 75 miles an hour and pushed everything out of the way, flashing his lights in people's mirrors. It must have gone on to 80 miles an hour. There was no writing on the side of the truck. Not a single word. No company name, nothing. It had to be a government killer truck!

He drove back onto the passing lane when it was safe. There was a hill and Peter's car picked up speed going down. He saw the license plate number of the truck and scribbled it down on a newspaper beside him.

The blue truck disappeared in the freeway haze of smog in the sunshine ahead.

He thought it was a deliberate attempt to kill him. "That fucking truck was sent," he later told a friend. "They just don't go that fast."

Peter went to see the postal inspector. "Where are you living?" was the inspector's first question.

"Around." *He knows where I'm living.*

"You have to be living somewhere."

"Can you help me? I'm having a lot of strange things happen."

"Like what?"

"A federal employee tried to kill me. Start with that."

"Well, that's not within the purview of the postal inspector's office. I don't think you ought to be talking like that, but you might want to speak with a United States Attorney in San Francisco."

"Thank you. I will."

"I'd be careful, if I were you. It only takes two doctors."

"What do you mean, two doctors?"

"Two doctors to declare you incompetent, and off you go to the loony bin."

"Did you hear anything about my missing mail?"

"We received a letter from a company about the statement you told us was missing. They deny it, but say that they sent another."

"What? Can I see it?"

The postal inspector showed him the letter from the company Peter had worked for. The last line of the letter said: "We hope that you will feel free to call us if you have any further questions." They dropped the nickel on him.

So that was how it worked.

"May I have a copy of this letter?"

"Yes." Always get a copy of everything. A hell of a lot of good it will do you if you try to do anything about anything.

As his class drew to a close, he knew that he had no job or anything to do. He tried to make his publishing effort grow, but it just flew real low. He applied to enter his small press—given birth by his torment—in book fairs in Berkeley and San Francisco, and was surprised when they accepted him. First there was the Berkeley fair, and then the San Francisco fair in August. He was making a noise like a publisher!

He talked to his class about the process of publishing, and knew that nobody in California had much if any chance of breaking into publishing in the East in those days, so the idea grew that they should produce a little book of their best stories. He tried to show them how to do it—and form their class into a publishing committee. It would have been a valuable experience. He wanted to leave them with something after he was gone.

At first they were steamed up about the plan, but when it came time to do anything at all, they took the safest route: They did nothing. No one would go to a printer to get estimates. No one would make lists of printers or typesetters in the area. No one would investigate the different methods of setting type. The person designated as editor gathered no stories from the others. They even failed to exchange their addresses so that they could remain in touch.

American writers were programmed to wait until it was handed to them. They waited for the *come*! The fact that so many great writers from Mark Twain to Fyodor Dostoevski had published themselves was lost on them.

He had a crazy idea, that he would leave a bit of a legacy there: a little book of their stories, which, in the end, represented some fine writing.

Each one had at some time during the period of the course he taught risen above themselves, outdoing themselves so to speak, and written something quite good. They showed each other what they could do in the middle of so much purple prose and trash. He thought that they should have a memory of it. Their work should be preserved.

But here he ran into an obstacle of the mind. People wanted to write, but the authoritarian state had locked them into looking towards publishers out in the great world, not towards themselves as publishers. Self-publishing had a stigma attached to it, of vanity and ego-centrism. Beside, self publishing was for radicals and leftists. It was rapidly shattering all of his allusions about costs and the need for centralized publishers, but the idea of self publishing was a subversive activity. So the work of his class was forever lost. Beside, self-publishers had little chance of competing or cracking distribution and marketing.

In addition, they sensed that they would become targets of government and police attention, and they did not want that. They were right.

Years later, I self published my first book on the JFK case, and it became a best seller and made some good money. There were some problems to solve to do this, and I had some help to make it happen. As you know, not much is easy.

The Chairman of the Department stuck by him, and wrote a letter of recommendation, which never got him another teaching job. The State evaluators and high school mentalities had done their dirty work.

"I am writing this letter in recommendation of Peter Casey. I have talked with his students and looked at their work. From the assignments they describe and the work they have produced, Peter appears to be an instructor who expects a great deal and yet one who provides the support needed for the realization of those expectations. One of my department colleagues who has formally evaluated Peter's teaching supports this observation. He found the student writing "superior to anything" students of his had produced that semester in the day section.

"I hope you have the opportunity to meet Peter. I think you will find him an interesting and unusual person."

He was out in the cold again.

Chapter 10

Peter talked around, trying to wangle a trip to Dallas. After the teaching job came to an end, he went to stay in Mendocino, a small town on the coast, where he had stayed before. There, a writer for the local newspaper took an interest in him, and she sent him to a friend of hers on the *San Francisco Chronicle*.

"What have you got?"

"I've got the names of three people I was told worked for the CIA, and my informant says that they may have handled or did handle the money paid to the assassins. He says the money was routed from Saigon to South America, and into New Orleans.

"And another man who worked for the CIA says that he saw the pay vouchers for Lee Harvey Oswald. Oswald worked for them."

"So that's why everyone thinks the CIA killed JFK?"

"Right," Peter said. "Only the clinker is that Oswald didn't do it...."

"That's what we all figure. What else have you got?"

"I have a contact in Dallas—someone who worked for Lyndon Johnson. He has been writing me. I don't know how much of his stuff gets through, but he says he has some leads. I think I really need to go down there and talk to him. I think it's big. Important."

"Well, I don't much believe in this conspiracy stuff, even if I don't think Oswald did it, but I know someone who is very interested in the case. I have a friend on another newspaper who might have the money to send you there. I think Oswald was framed after the fact." This editor, like so many who ventured to think about the case, never thought through what he was saying and how dumb it was. It took a great deal of planning to frame Oswald. He had to be set up, and planted in the building where the shots were claimed to have come from.

The contact was made. Peter was put on a plane that night for Dallas, although he did not have much in the way of clothes and just wore jeans. What luxury! Sitting down in the plane was like a breath of fresh air. It put a new perspective on life to have such a good experience. It was cleansing.

The pretty flight attendants doted on him the same as everyone else, if not a little more attentive. He was bizarre in his Mountain Man outfit. Actually, years later, someone would accuse him of being a "detriment" to the case. The man who said it turned out to be one of the biggest frauds around. At least Peter was honest.

Later, Peter's integrity would be impugned however they could get something on him with frame-ups and set-ups. The new game was to publicly discrediting him because he was rocking the boat.

Those hours in the plane took him away from so much, and he was able to clear out the cobwebs, along with having a scotch and water. Only too soon, the plane ride was over. The fear had already set in. He was afraid of what he was going to try to do. Afraid of going around that violent city asking questions. Afraid of Dallas.

Peter met his contact after some searching around. The contact, a reporter, was drunk.

The man may have worked for Lyndon Johnson once, but the experience was rapidly destroying him. He was one of those who never got over the assassination, and was drinking himself to death, like some of those who had been in Kennedy's Secret Service detail. Not that LBJ might have had something to do with Kennedy's death, and a man who worked for him might be setting a trap for Peter Casey.

"I was a reporter at the time Kennedy was killed," he said. "We started knocking on doors. I had a friend, another reporter. He still works for the *Dallas Morning News*, and follows the case. He still writes about it. We went to see many people. I talked to Jack Ruby at the trial and he said to me, 'It is the most bizarre conspiracy in the history of the world.'

"We went to see Oswald's landlady and she told us about the police car coming by the house and honking, when Oswald went there just after the assassination. That might have been Tippit. We talked to witnesses who were at the scene of the Tippit murder, and they said that two men did the shooting. Oswald didn't seem to fit the description. We talked to the manager of the YMCA where Oswald stayed, and he said that he used to eat with Oswald. He had a great deal of information about Oswald, about how much money he had or didn't have, but we were never able to follow it up. Somebody shut him up and he wouldn't talk to us anymore."

"Well, you said that you had some information.... That's why I came here...."

For the next three days, Peter tried to get him to arrange the interviews, but failed. The man drank, and hung Peter on a hook in his apartment. Maybe he was testing Peter. But he did nothing for several days. Peter's money ran short. After all, maybe Peter might be from the CIA. That was what they were all afraid of. The CIA was everyone's bogey man.

Finally he was sent to another reporter and there given some leads—people to talk to. Peter went to the lawyer for some of the policemen and there got a big story. But like so much else in the case, it would disappear into a vacuum tube somewhere, down the Black Hole of the case. What did it matter?

The only thing to do was to gather it all together in a compendium of the evidence for the future. They would never be able to get anywhere with it in their lifetimes, he thought. All they could do was leave a more complete record than the Warren Commission had done for future historians.

The material wasn't startling, but it was pretty strong. There, he also reread the testimony of the doctors at Dallas about the head wounds. Dr. Gene Akin had said that the "back of the right occipital-parietal portion of his head was shattered, with brain substance protruding." Dr. Robert McClelland said that ".... the right posterior portion of the skull had been blasted.... some of the occipital bone being fractured in its lateral half and this sprung open the bones in such a way that you could actually look down into the skull cavity itself and see that probably a third or so, at least, of the brain tissue, posterior cerebral tissue and some of the cerebellar tissue had been blasted out."

Peter flew back to San Francisco, enjoying the momentary luxury of the flight again, and having a couple of scotches. He felt that the small amount of research he had done and the report he brought back with him was valuable. It was indeed a small group to which he belonged, still on the periphery of the important people among the critics. He had no ambition there. Peter sought only to help expose the crimes, not to make a name for himself. He hadn't been caught up in the fire of the investigation yet, as would happen later. It would become a consuming fire.

Peter made his report to the people that sent him, having taken careful notes, and wrote a summary before he left The City. He wondered if the news organization they worked for was in reality controlled or run by the Texas faction in the CIA. By David Atlee Phillips, or whomever it was. When he went to Washington a few months later, when Congress established the Assassination Committee, they would cut his legs out from under him, after sending him there.

It was a deep game. Phillips was from Ft. Worth, and was the Chief of the Western Hemisphere Division of the CIA. He was a propaganda specialist and was stationed in Mexico City at the time of the alleged visit by Lee Harvey Oswald, the accused assassin of the President. Phillips was the one who got all over the news in the *Washington Post* when the House Select Committee on Assassinations was set up in 1976, and he personally tried to destroy that committee.

Phillips was running scared, but he moved with the ferocity, speed and skill of a crocodile.

The one thing they had to hide from the Senate Intelligence Committee, Carl Bernstein wrote in "The CIA and the Media" in the *Rolling Stone*, was the fact that the CIA pretty much controlled the press.

Woodward and Bernstein ought to know! They had uncovered the cover-up of the Watergate break-in and brought President Nixon down.

Chapter 11

▼

"We have the forms of institutions, rather than the reality. Form masquerades as substance. Our Congress is not a congress, the unions not unions, and the newspapers are not newspapers. It is impossible to organize and it cannot be efficient. In such conditions it is impossible to be just."

—So wrote Scherer Garcia.

Peter drove to San Francisco to try to get help. Casey called the ACLU. "Please help me."

"What do you do?"

"I'm a writer."

"We can't help you." What, are writers beyond help? Off limits?

"But, don't you understand? My life is being destroyed."

"We're just interested in street vagrancy right now. We can't have any interest in private suits."

"But, they tried to blow me up!"

"Who?"

"The government."

"We can't help you." They only did the up-front high profile cases. No one in the middle could get help. His type of First Amendment case didn't matter. It was impossible.

"My God, don't you know what is happening to me? If it's happening to *one* person, if you let this happen to *one* person, then there is no hope for this country!"

"What makes you think you're so special?" He could almost hear them laughing. He pleaded with them, and shivered in the phone booth by the ocean. There was heavy fog, and the air was chilled. He was afraid, alone, without support. Frightened beyond telling. He was afraid of what would happen next, close to hysteria.

"Help me, *please*.... I was nearly killed by a Federal agent a few months ago. All sorts of things are happening to me."

"Like what?"

"My mail is being opened.... My mail just disappears.... I tried to start a little publishing company, and they just destroyed it on the spot. They ruined my distribution for the book...." He saw how futile it was. How ridiculous it sounded.

"I was black-listed."

"What?"

He choked on the words. "Black-listed. They said to me, '*You will never be published again. We can play pretty rough!*'" Tears sprang to his eyes as he said the awful words that never stopped ringing in his ears and had destroyed his life. He was a broken man, without money or hope. The words had killed the hope in him for the one thing that mattered.

It was cold in the phone booth and there was rain in the air. They didn't bother to put doors on the phone booths anymore, and soon would disappear altogether. His legs quaked and shivered. "They tried to kill me. The man worked with the CIA or the DIA, I don't know. I know that it sounds fantastic, but it happened. They tried to blow up my car."

"How do you know he worked with the CIA?"

"Because I worked with him." He forgot to say that they had worked for the Department of Agriculture. He always forgot to say that. It did not occur to him that everything came out wrong when he tried to deal with events since the blacklisting. Now the ACLU thought that *he*, Peter, worked for the CIA, and that this was just a matter for the CIA. They turned it over to the CIA, turned him over to the CIA! Of course, an outfit like the ACLU would have been co-opted long before by their enemies.

Numerous federal agencies provided cover for agents of one kind or another from several other agencies.

"Will you go see some people in Berkeley that might be able to help you?"

"Who?"

"The Bay Area Lawyers for the Arts, or BALA, as they call themselves. They might help." The title of the organization appealed to him. But he misread everything, often investing hope in that which could or would do nothing. One drills a lot of dry holes that way.

"All right," Peter responded. The ACLU man gave him the number and address of BALA.

First, before going over to Berkeley, he went to the Federal Building in San Francisco and located the Department of Justice there. They would help him, he thought. But the *Department of Justice* was just a euphemism. It was a sick joke on all those people who thought to turn to it as a last resort for the injustice they had suffered.

"Who do you wish to see?" the receptionist asked.

"A lawyer."

"Which lawyer?"

"A United States Attorney."

"Well, you have to have an appointment. You just can't walk in off the street. Which United States Attorney did you wish to see?"

"I don't know...."

He was shaking, frightened. He sensed danger and was almost out of control. Seeing this, they figured he had a bomb or a machine gun and was going to tear up the place. Terror had done its evil work on Peter. Once, when he was like this, he had gone into Senator Edward Kennedy's campaign office and tried to talk to them about the conspiracy that murdered his brothers, tried to warn him that it was still in place. But Kennedy's staffers figured the fearful young man with the wild eyes had a bomb under his coat, or a gun, and they called the Secret Service, who came and interviewed him, after a search. They kept interviewing him, as he certainly seemed to be a suspect.

"Please, I have driven hundreds of miles to come here. Can't you help me? I was nearly killed by a Federal agent. All sorts of things are being done to me. My mail is being taken. I'm being threatened, and violence was done...."

"Please have a seat." Peter sat down, quite distracted. Numerous people came in and out, and many lawyers, well dressed, carrying briefcases and picking up their message memos at the desk. They exchanged greetings and smiles with one another, and put their hands on one another's back in a confidential, chatty way, controlling each other in the interim, holding one to the other in bonds of shared secrets and work. Casey was an outsider.

He felt as though he were being watched. A man in not such an expensive suit as the others were wearing—with a moustache and a bulge that looked like a gun, stood about, not talking much to anyone, making glances at Peter. He observed Peter off and on for some time, making him very nervous, until Peter was certain that the man had been sent by the receptionist to take care of him. And, true, Peter had a tormented look in his eyes. There was confusion there, and hurt and anger, desperation in his eyes. He must have looked like a madman in his jeans and woolen Pendleton shirt, beard and heavy mountain hiking boots. His beard had not been trimmed in six months. He was not like *them*, so he must have been crazy.

He smelled a little, too.

He would go crazy, too, if this kind of nightmare kept up. Finally, the U.S. Marshall with the moustache came over to him and asked him whom he wished to see.

"A U.S. Attorney."

"Well, come with me, then." He was led downstairs on an elevator and to an entrance that said, "Federal Bureau of Investigation."

"This is not the Department of Justice."

"The Bureau of Investigation is under the Department of Justice."

"It isn't where I wanted to go."

"They prosecute cases. The FBI prepares them, and the U.S. Attorney prosecutes them. You have to talk to the FBI first." Peter was led into a small office near the front door. He began to wonder if he was going to be arrested and prosecuted for going there. Maybe they wanted him for something?! The man inside was sort of the officer of the day, rather pleasant, and Peter calmed down. He was in quite a state.

"What is your problem?"

"I want to see a U.S. Attorney."

"I'm afraid you must talk to us before you can see them."

"Is that in the United States Code?"

"You have to talk to us."

"I want to see a United States Attorney." He was afraid of them now. Real afraid.

"You have to talk to us."

"I want to go now."

"No."

"What if I don't want to talk to you?"

"Then you are free to leave."

There was a long silence. Peter strove to untie the knot the man had just made in his brain. Tried to unblock the acute anxiety block....

"I'm afraid. I was nearly killed a few months ago. I am blacklisted. My mail is being opened. My mail disappears."

"If you are having trouble with your mail, you should talk to the postal inspectors."

"I have."

"Why don't you write the U.S. Attorney about it?" He was a nut but he couldn't face it.

Peter did appear to be mad. They would never understand. Once a person appeared to be unstable, they lost their rights. So the trick was to destabilize them.

"There are federal laws being violated here," he went on, his voice catching. "My mail is being opened."

"How do you know that it is being opened?"

"I can tell. They come taped, or it is obvious that they have been steamed open and resealed. The corners are torn in exactly the same way. The letters are crinkled inside, as though they had been pulled from the torn corner of the envelope."

"Did you write your Congressman about it?"

"Yes. They take those letters too." Then, with a start, he recalled that the Congressman was a strong law-and-order man, a Reagan and Nixon man, a Conservative hardly likely to support the law as applied to a citizen under surveillance and destabilization.

"Did you write anyone else?"

"Yes. I wrote Senator Tunney." They were finding out everything about him—who his contacts were. What was Dostoyevsky's book, *The Idiot*, about? He must be The Idiot, the misguided idealist, still believing that somewhere he might find Justice, except that he did not take offense.

"Why was I brought down here? I want to talk to a United States Attorney."

"We investigate the cases first." The man was going by the book, but Peter was too distraught to grasp the procedure.

"But, I have reason to talk to them...."

"The receptionist said that you looked unstable. She was afraid of you. We get a lot of nuts around here."

"I'm not a nut!" But he was! He tried to see himself as they saw him.

Nobody in their right mind would try to resist, try to get help. There was no help.

"I didn't say that you were." Peter excused himself, frightened that he had told them so much, that now they had him in a file somewhere, a data bank, for trying to get help. Peter went upstairs again, and tried once more to talk to a U.S. Attorney. This time, as he came down the hall, he saw that there was a section of lawyers outside the main entrance. A sign said "Antitrust." He could fit his problem—at least for a little while—into that slot. He went into the first office he came to. "May I speak to a lawyer?"

"Which one? We have many!" The receptionist fixed him with a fiercely false smile, pleased with her sense of humor.

"Mr. Donovan." He had seen the name on a door as he came in.

"Just a moment."

An attorney was called, and Peter was invited into an office, and was interviewed. "It's an antitrust case," Peter began. "My troubles started with illegal business practices in the industry...." But his troubles had no beginning and no end. Everyone has troubles.

"Were they deceitful?"

"Yes."

"Deceptive? Did they keep their word?"

"No. Their word meant nothing. They had no honor. Their written contracts meant nothing. They just got control of your ideas and ran. They took your property and ran, saying they were doing you a favor."

"They are in business to make money," the government lawyer said, with sympathy. "The law means nothing to them, and they will push the law as far as they can, until they are called on it."

"Can't someone do something?"

"I don't know."

"Will you help me?"

"I don't know. Who sent you here? How did you happen to come to me or ask about me?"

"I just walked in off the street, trying to see someone."

"I don't think I can help you."

"Doesn't anyone care? How can I get help? I was nearly murdered by a federal agent. How can I get help?" His voice broke. "I am so afraid...."

"I don't believe that anyone tried to kill you."

There it was again. They didn't believe him, and he lost all credibility. He never had it.

"Isn't it a crime for someone to threaten my printer?"

"I imagine it is. I'd have to look it up."

"Isn't it a crime to blacklist someone? To defraud them of their property and then blacklist them?"

"I imagine so. I don't know that blacklisting is a crime."

"Isn't it a form of assault? Of mental torment? Don't you think there must be a law to cover mental torment? Isn't it a crime to close someone out of the free market place of ideas? Wasn't that an antitrust case?"

"That was the Red Lion case."

"There was another Federal case against the publishing industry in 1967: illegal price fixing."

"I didn't know about that. That was before I was here."

"The government won that one too. A consent decree. The industry gave up. Everything they do is illegal. The contracts are illegal and coercive. It's all crooked and illegal. Don't you see, they had to shut me up. I can't imagine any business so crooked as this one. What in hell is the First Amendment for, if the media is so rigged?"

"Let me ask you something.... Did you say all this to your publisher at the start? Later on? That is sure a good way to turn them off and turn them against you."

"*No*! I never said a word to them while we were working together. It was later, when they came down on me. They destroyed me on the day I finished a book for them...." The terrible words sprang up in his mind, freezing him.

"Anything else?"

At least he was talking to somebody, getting it out, even if the man was not listening. But he was listening. He had not thrown him out on the spot, or not responded at all. But what good did it do? Peter had run around like a mad man talking to this person and that, telling his story, asking for help, and there was no end to it. There was no way to set right the terrible crime. It was just like the nightmare of child abuse and all that followed with that. There was nothing anyone could do. He had to simply keep running and try to outrun it and find a way to do better, to succeed after all. He had to win through....

"The contracts everyone must sign are a kind of indentured servitude. And the CIA is into everything. Here, look at this," Peter said, flashing a newspaper article at the lawyer, excited that he had found an antitrust lawyer to talk to. "The CIA admitted to having over 400 journalists, editors and so on, on the payroll!"

"The CIA?"

"Yes. That's what we're talking about. They control it. That's governmental intervention into the press, and it's wrong! It's illegal...and that is what I ran into. My boss' roommate was a CIA assassin...."

Peter came up short. The enormity of all that he was saying struck him back like a blow, and he saw how crazy it sounded. Yes, the CIA and the DIA were into killing people. Right then, the San Francisco papers had carried a story about the Navy's school for assassins.

The government had plotted to kill, or killed foreign leaders it did not like. It had invaded the sovereignty of other nations and manipulated or controlled their internal affairs. Why should not the government do that to its own citizens?

"Who else have you talked to?"

"I went to the ACLU. They asked me to see the Bay Area Lawyers for the Arts."

"I think you should try to see if they can help you. I don't believe I can. I can't mess with the CIA. I am just a little person. What you have here is a can of worms. You want to fight an industry and you can't. Not one man alone. You have to have a lot of help. I don't think the government can help you because, as you say, it is the government you might have to fight. We are just little people, and they are big people."

The ACLU, then, was turning over its minutes to the FBI, and lists of its members. It was controlled and watched, run to some extent, by the FBI, by the government.

Everything was a cover to make it look like we had rights, had *law*, had the Constitution. Maybe we aren't any different from Mexico or Russia.

This kind of thing destroys first the culture and then the political fabric of a nation.

Chapter 12

It had taken years, most of his adult life, to write books. While Peter was working in New York, he took six of his manuscripts and walked into a publisher's office cold. He didn't know what else to do. Years before it seemed like the "casting couch" was the only way in the literary world in New York. Either you laid down with an agent, or you got nowhere.

He would try again and again trying to find a way to break in. But it was a closed shop to straights in those days, it seemed. Much of the publishing world was run by the gay community, and they were very hostile to guys like him. They wanted tolerance but they were intolerant. They were not very mature, either.

But neither was he. Peter was for many years still the victim of vast child abuse by his mother, and it was the hardest thing in the world to break out. The hardest thing in the world to get over.

"Do you have an appointment?"

"No."

"Whom do you wish to see?"

"An editor."

"Any editor?"

"Yes."

"You can't see anyone without an appointment."

"Even a published author?" he whispered, knowing that she would ask him who his publisher had been. One question would lead to another, phone calls would be made, and his effort would be futile.

"Are you published?" That was what they had to know. It was the acid test that told them if he had been bought and paid for and how he handled it. It told them if he was docile, obedient, met his deadlines, did what he was told, accepted editing. Maybe if they could steal from him. Maybe have him cooperate in theft from the work of others. Render "treatments" and so on.

"Yes."

"A book?"

"Yes." His eyes started to see things in a haze. His vision half clouded over, and he was in danger of an anxiety block. The receptionist could see that his eyes were glazed. His blood pressure went through the roof. She just thought he was on drugs. He was so unkempt.... Maybe she took pity on him.

"Just a moment. Have a seat. I'll call someone for you."

A secretary soon came out, or rather someone saying she was an editorial assistant. "What can I do for you?" Peter wanted to run, to cry, to plead. "Please help me—I've been black-listed," he said. Peter thrust the six novels in front of her. "Do you understand how much work this is?"

"I work hard too," she said. "I've got nothing to show for it."

"What company black-listed you?" they asked. He told them. Peter brought the issue up because it would come out sooner or later, and he thought it was best to get it out in the open.

"Isn't there an editor here somewhere?" he asked. She disappeared and brought back a man who turned out to be the editor-in-chief. They were intrigued with what he said about blacklisting. Much later, too late, after many months of waiting, he learned that the editor-in-chief was a writer and had the same publisher that had black-listed Peter for his own book.

He'd walked into another trap, but had no way of knowing it just then. Not until coming across a remaindered copy of the editor's book in a store.

"I've been black-listed," he said.

"What did you do? How could that happen?"

"I don't know. I didn't do anything."

"You must have done something." The editor didn't ask what the company had done to him, just what he might have done.

"I sued them."

"That will do it. Why?"

"They said, '*You will never be published again. We can play pretty rough!*'" The terrible and painful words stabbed at him as they were uttered. The psychic murder that day years before would never leave him. The day he had thrown his manuscript across the park in front of his editor with bitter tears in his eyes, and walked away, leaving the editor to collect the pages from all over the place.

"Why did they say that? What did you do to them?"

"It's what they did to me."

"Well, publishers are in business to make money. To sell books. What happened that led to this?"

"They changed my book."

"Publishers edit books. Is that what bothered you? Editing?"

"**No!** Not at all." He could barely speak about this. "I wrote a novel, and they insisted that it be put into the first person. It was to be my first published book. I said I would not do it. One day they gave it back to me put into the first person. It was too personal, you know. It had to do with child abuse. And some of the things were not true, which they had me write. I didn't mind doing it, if it was a novel—about somebody else, but to say that *I* did those things, and so on, was all wrong…It was no longer a novel—an artistic work."

Peter felt like the load he was carrying was crushing him to death in that rich office in downtown Manhattan. It felt like death itself telling this story one more time. The pain of it was insupportable. He had been *killed* emotionally by the threat made to him. It had destroyed his identity—his sense of self.

But the editor-in-chief seemed kind. He took Peter's books, and Peter waited three months. During that time, Peter did not get any word at all. He waited quietly, and did not bother them or call, afraid of upsetting the apple cart. He was working at the hospital where he applied to work in the heart research program, and made a stab at being someone else in life. But there was no joy in the job, which again seemed to radically twist his tenuous identity. The job and the white lab coat he wore did not work out so well. The strange events began to happen on that job, too, after he finally called the editor to find out what was happening with the manuscripts he submitted. He had seen the editor's book in the bookstore and knew that they had the same publisher. It was another dry hole, and the publisher's world and its old boy network was so tightly knit, he would never overcome what had happened to close him out. It was as though he had killed his own children or something.

But his books were his children, and they had been killed.

When he got on the phone with the editor, Peter played him along. It was all small talk and he knew the editor knew why he was calling, but he wasn't going to bring it up.

"Where are you working?" the editor-in-chief asked him.

Peter did not answer at first, sensing danger. He was afraid to say, afraid he'd lose that job, but finally answered. He did not understand how vicious and cruel people really are. He just could not understand that a network of people were out to get him.

His apartment had been broken into the moment he had moved into it. So many rotten things happened.

Finally Peter asked about his books. The editor-in-chief invited Peter down to talk, and for a little while he was hopeful. He took a couple of hours off from his job at the hospital and grabbed a subway, excited, thinking he was finally going to break the chains that bound him.

"Well," the editor-in-chief said, "if you could convert this story into the first person...." He was talking about Peter's sea novel, the book that Peter had so carefully nurtured and protected all of those years.

Peter froze, the room went black, all the fuses of his mind blowing out. He sat there, gazing past the man at the photo of a lovely woman on the desk in front of a fine large and secure house in the suburbs, out the window down upon Central Park, at a superb view of the city, the sky-scrapers from many stories above, at green trees far below in the vast expanse of the

Park in the center of the city. He thought of Lincoln Center and the New York State Theatre, of the ballet and Georges Balanchine and Gelsey Kirkland—and all they wanted him to do was write in the first person! All they wanted to do was rape and pervert, warp and twist his best writing. To be a public spectacle.

"No," he said quietly.

The editor asked him to do some revisions. No guidance was given. Peter went home and worked on the book for a week, gazing at it, trying to see what might be wrong with it. There wasn't anything wrong with it. The book did not have a plot with a twist like *Jaws* or a phoney story like the *Poseidon Adventure*. It was true to life. It was a *good story*. Its style was just different, that's all.

Then he resubmitted the book to the man at the publishing house. "What are you going to do?" Peter finally asked. He had lost his job at the hospital by then. He was down in the dumps. The editor was just playing with him all along.

"About what?"

"About the book I gave you."

"We can't publish it, of course."

"Why not?"

"You don't want to convert it into the first person."

"You mean you would publish it if I did?"

"I didn't say that."

"This is pretty hard to take."

"I can't understand you saying that. I'm offering you a chance. Well, I have to get back to work. Call me anytime. Maybe we can work something out."

They were trying to break him.

He lost the job, and by the end of November, Peter had played out his string in New York. He found that he would not receive unemployment insurance for reasons that weren't clear. The Forest Service had strange ways of accounting that prevented him from getting what he should have, and that also prevented him from collecting from his last job at the hospital. The law read that a certain amount had to be *paid* to him in a certain quarter, and some of the checks he'd received were outside the quarter—just enough to deny him unemployment insurance. That must have been why they were so intent on firing him by a certain day.

He was broke and tried to get a job, but failed. Serious economic recession began to strike down the nation about then. Peter went back to see the editor. "What can I write for you that you might be interested in?"

"I'm interested in the West. I'm from Montana and I love it out there. Do you have any ideas about that?"

They discussed a story about the Rocky Mountains Peter had in mind. He had always wanted to drive north and south along the mountains, exploring the many small towns off the beaten path.

Peter went back to see the editor two or three times, while submitting his work elsewhere. They still had his sea story. "What will you do with the novel?" he asked.

"I'll see if my friend over at Pocket Books will take it as an original paperback."

It was agreed that Peter would go West, in December. He could no longer make his rent in New York, anyway. He was given no instructions, no money, no promises, nothing less than to write about the Rockies, or "have you seen Studs Turkel's new book *Working*? See if you can get a job in the mines...."

Yes, with heart and lung disease they would exile him to the mines at high altitudes in mid-winter. It was a trap, a wild goose chase, a trick, but Peter did not know it. He suspected it but had to take the chance. He suspected that he was being set up, but he had to grasp at straws.

"Stick to small towns off the beaten path," the editor-in-chief told him, sending him off into the unknown in the dead of winter. "Be brave," were his only instructions.

This editor lived by the old cowboy code of the west which taught one how to be a man. It was fit for the range, but not for the modern world, and said nothing in the face of the great and corrupt powers arrayed against all of us, the great conspiracies against humanity.

Peter had to take a chance that it was real, and wanted to believe and to trust *someone*. He decided to trust this man, who may have owed his career to the same publisher which had black-listed Peter. He had seemed to be nice to Peter when Peter needed a friend. What a fool he was.

One final blow was to strike him before he had packed up and gone from New York that December. He had submitted his books to a publisher that had kept them for one year. Later the publisher was listed as a CIA front. They kept his books for a full year and said nothing, and then the editor wrote him, saying "I do understand your frustration over the length of time that I have had your manuscripts." Then the editor said something that Peter had not been aware of, and this cost him the year. He was told, "When you chose to leave them with me, I indicated that I did not intend to publish fiction, and that I was just getting started and therefore you should be warned that patience on your part would be required.

"I have given your manuscripts my most serious consideration and regret to say that I do not find them publishable in their present form. You need a brilliant and powerful editor. I am not that person. I unfortunately am not as familiar as I would like to be with the bright new fiction editors. Consequently, I am not, alas, able to suggest someone to work with you."

This was how Peter ended up camping in the forest and the snow in January in California. He had to go to someplace where he could safely camp and knew his way around, and try to recover.

He took one last night to walk back from a friend's loft near the Bowery. It was snowing and bitter cold, and he came to four sleeping men laid out on the sidewalk with no boxes or anything else to protect them. One by one he dragged or helped each of the men inside the doorway of a building where a door was unlocked, so that they could be in the hallway. The owner would not like that, but then he must be used to it.

Chapter 13

▼

Peter went over to Berkeley to see if he could get help from the lawyers for the arts group. He saw one of Charles Manson's girls on the street putting up posters for a televised jail interview of their leader and hero. At first Peter did not realize that they were Manson girls. Evil was not at first evident. Instead, they drew attention to themselves with hardened nipples showing through their thin blouses.

They were little, and they lived, walked, and radiated eroticism.

She was very pretty, but quite short. She had light blond hair, wore bangs and a white cotton blouse. Maybe only five feet tall at the most. She was putting up a poster, she and her equally tiny girlfriend, on the wall of a building on Durant Street, near Telegraph Avenue. The poster announced that an interview with Charles Manson, convicted mass murderer, would be on T.V.

They were strange and compelling—crossed with wholesome, almost childish looks and erotic magnetism. He was drawn to them, almost hypnotically. The girls vibrated sex and psychic power. They were evil. Satanic.

"What's that?" Peter asked.

"Are you the law?"

"No!" he laughed, nervously. She was cute and pretty. Nice breasts and hard nipples. His dick usually led him around in a case like this, and no *telling* the trouble they might have brought. But then, a lovely blond girl living at the Moony Church up the street had also got him into their orbit for a short time, using her youth, beauty, touch and all her whiles to get him to come over for dinner with their group, and that led to threats and violence up north when they whisked her away to their guarded compound in the middle of nowhere. She made the mistake of liking Peter when she was only supposed to be walking on the street as bait and not get involved. She was an accomplished hooker for sure! At least he was able to locate her and tell her parents where she was—and warn them of the riflemen at the gate.

Then he noticed the X carved between the eyes of each of the Manson girls on their foreheads above the bridge of their noses. "You want to know the truth, don't you? All they tell us are lies."

His attention was drawn away for a moment. When he turned back they were gone. They simply evaporated. He wanted to talk a bit more, to learn something more, but they actually disappeared. Poof, and they were gone, like a puff of smoke.

Then he realized with a frightened start who they were.

How gruesome! The Manson girls right there on the street. They looked wholesome, but they radiated heat, sex and desire. There wasn't a man who was a man who would not want to fuck them, until he knew who they really were.

This was shortly before one of the girls he had seen took a shot at President Ford. Maybe she was "Squeaky Fraum". Maybe somebody in the government put them up to it. Maybe the attacks on Ford were only for show, to get him some support and sympathy, having been appointed by Tricky Dick, and then pardoning Nixon. Maybe they were provocateurs. Maybe they and the Moore woman, who also took a shot at Ford around that time, were put up to it to let Ford know that there was a *secret team* in the government that was the real boss.

Maybe they did it to every president, one way or another.

Then there were the Children of God. There weren't entirely recluses, but hooked men for money, or tried to. "The Family." If a person was in the habit of responding to appeals for help, it was easy to fall into a dangerous web.

He went to see a lawyer at the Bay Area Lawyers For The Arts.

"What is your problem?"

"I...." He froze. The words stuck to his lips, and he froze with fear, in an acute anxiety block. Peter had told his story so many times. Someday, he would have to put it aside, bury it, and try to start fresh.

"It's all lies," he said. "All they tell us are lies."

The young lawyer was patient and waited. After awhile, Peter told his story again.

"We will help you, but I want you to see someone first. It is imperative that we get you out from under your legal problems so that kind of strain goes away."

"Yes. What will you do?"

"I'll speak to a lawyer about helping you, but first it is imperative that you see a friend of mine. Will you?"

"Sure. Who is it?"

"Here, I'll write it down for you." He scribbled a name on his card.

"Is this a psychiatrist?"

"Yes."

"I don't need a psychiatrist."

"Maybe he can give you some medicine that will relieve you of your tension..."

"Did the ACLU call you?"

"Yes."

"What did they say?"

"They said that you had some problems they thought we could help you with over here."

"What kind of problems?"

"Legal and emotional problems."

"I have legal problems with this thing—with this society. With life. I may be emotionally upset, but it is because of what is being done to me. You are a lawyer: Don't just treat the symptoms of disease. Get at the cause. Sue the mother-fuckers."

"We can't. That's not our function. Beside, it costs a lot of money."

"What is your function?"

"We raise funds for the arts, and so on."

"But can't you care about what an industry does to one artist? To all of them, with illegal publishing contracts? What right have conglomerates to be in this industry?"

"We haven't established that the contracts are illegal...."

"Oh, you have heard about that issue?"

"I heard a little, yes. I think your union, what is it? The Author's Guild? They say the contract is illegal, but that doesn't make it so."

"Well, it is."

"I promise you, if you will see this doctor, we will help you. You have got to get out from under the emotional and legal load you're carrying."

"You mean my suit against the industry?"

"Is that what it is?"

"Well, it's actually against one company, but it will apply to the whole industry if I get a favorable decision."

"Who is your lawyer?"

"I haven't got one. It's in court in *pro se*."

"You need the person I want you to see. Will you go see him?"

After awhile Peter responded. "All right, I'll go see him."

"Fine."

Peter went to see the doctor that day. The psychiatrist operated out of one of those slick, expensive doctor's building that only the patient's insurance company could pay for, where one parked underneath the building. The place stank of sterility and control. It was full of psychologists, psychiatrists, and neurologists. The joint would come down real fast in an earthquake.

The doctor, Maynard Williams, was right out of *The Search for the Manchurian Candidate, Operation Mind Control,* and *The Mind Manipulator.*

The doc sat back with all the savoir faire of a snake oil pitch-man playing a waiting game, like a spider catching an insect in its web. Cat and mouse.

All a shrink had to do, or anyone knowing the technique of a shrink and asking those same questions, was to play a waiting game, and a victim reveals his weaknesses. Once his weaknesses are out, that person is ripe for control. After all, the goal in those years was to get a lid on radicalism and free thought, of criticism of the established order of society. Everyone was afraid of that. Much of the turmoil of the Sixties had started in Berkeley, except for the black Civil Rights movement, and Berkeley was the place where the forces of mind control were tried out and clamped down on people like Peter. First, they had to be sucked in.

Peter's mistake was trying to write omniscient novels at a time in the late Sixties when the controllers of the country wanted writers to lead youth to self concern, when books (novels?) like *Stop Time* were to be the model of a new self centered youth. Anything but concern for *others* and their problems. They refocused an entire nation and its colleges, by 1970, away from social issues. Or else. And they did it right in the middle of a war everyone had enough of. Anyone who questioned authority was a target.

This guy did not look like a doctor. He looked like an FBI agent. He lacked compassion. He had never heard of the Hippocratic oath. Was he one of those many people in the medical profession that dropped drugs in people's wine or coffee to see what happened? One who experimented with stelazine, thorazine or ibocaine on the innocent and helpless?

"What's the problem?" the doctor asked.

"I need a lawyer."

"Tell me a little about your background. Maybe I can help you better if I know a little more about you."

"What do you want to know?"

"Tell me about your childhood."

"No."

"Why not?"

"I don't want to."

"It would really help me if I knew more about your childhood," Dr. Williams said.

"I thought you wanted to help *me*."

"I do. Whatever gave you the idea I did not want to help you?"

"I hear this word 'help' a lot, and I don't see happening what I need. And, I don't think knowing about my childhood has got anything to do with it. I had some severe trauma then and a lot more recently. It's post-traumatic stress syndrome."

"Well then, we have to treat that. Treat the symptoms, if you will."

"What with? Pills?"

"Perhaps. There are marvelous medicines for everything these days."

"I just guess I'm a paranoid. Maybe a paranoid or schizo. Maybe that's how I got the idea."

"You are very perceptive. We can treat your paranoia. How long have you had this condition? I treat many paranoids in Berkeley."

"Probably a long time." He was about to fly over the cuckoo's nest.

"Tell me, did you get along with your mother?"

"Oh, yes, now and then. Maybe once or twice." Never more than an hour.

There was a long and deadly silence. It was planned that way. The psychotherapist sat quietly, waiting. The idea is to keep waiting. Finally someone is forced to speak. In this case, the silence was very long.

"Well, it's time to go now," the doctor said.

"What will you do?"

"What do you mean?"

"What will you do to help me? The lawyer that sent me here said that if I saw you, you will help me."

"I *will* help you. The process has already started. Why don't you come and see me in three days, say on Friday?"

"See you about what?"

"We'll have another session. By the way, do you have medical insurance?"

"No."

"Do you have state Medicaid?"

"No."

"Well, we'll work out something. How much can you afford?"

"For what?"

"For this hour," Williams said.

"You want me to pay you now? Pay you for this?"

"No. I meant, for this hour that I will set aside for you."

"You want to give me therapy?" He wanted to ask how much they were going to pay *him* for going there....

"I think that if you are going to get relief from the emotional problems that you're under, you have to get out from under the legal burden you have with your suit against the industry, and so on. I think this hour can be very helpful to you. Can you afford twenty dollars an hour?"

"No."

"Why not? You have to get used to paying for things. You probably have gotten through much of your life living on the fringe. You can't keep getting things for free. You can't keep living like the rest of these people. You have too much ability for that."

"What people?"

"The people living on the streets here. Hippies and Beatniks or whatever they are." Beatniks Peter identified with, but not *hippies*!

"I don't have a job."

"Can't your family help you?"

"How? *Help me*?!" The "doctor" struck a raw nerve—*family*.

"With the money to pay for this hour. Can't you get $20 from them?"

"I don't want them to pay for this hour."

"Do you have a family? Can't they help you?"

"Yes, I have a family.... Christ, they've been killing me!"

"Where does your mother live? I can get in touch with her...." Christ, the doctor was closing in now. He knew just what button to push.

"She doesn't want anybody to know."

"Where does your father live?"

"I think you want to call them."

"I —oh, no! I would never do anything like that without your permission. I just wondered how you are getting along with your family."

"Just great. We're in touch all the time. I love them dearly," he lied.

"Then why are you here?"

"What do you mean?"

"Why are you seeing a psychiatrist?"
"Sir, I was *sent* here!"
"But, *why?*"
"Because I must have been traumatized."
"Did you feel rejected as a child?"

He did not answer. Peter sat quietly, wanting to laugh, wanting to scream at the man, "*You fool!*" But he did not. Of course he had been rejected viciously, brutally by his mother for years, until he ran away for good when he was fourteen.

"I can't help you if I can't talk to your parents. I need to know more about your past. How do I know that what you are telling me is the truth, that the side of yourself that you present here is *you*? You might be on the run from the law, for all I know."

"I'm not on the run. I've never been in trouble."

"You are in trouble now."

"I meant in trouble with the law. I've never been in trouble with the law."

"Well, I need to know what made you the way you are."

"I've had some terrible things happen to me...." He fell silent and the doctor said nothing. But Peter did not go on. He froze with acute pain, with mental anguish of knowing there was no way out. The only thing was to keep running. To run and run and run until somehow it would all go away. And somehow, it did, but it took many more years and new passions that took his mind off of the past.

"Well, it's time to go."

"I know," Peter responded. He thought he would torture the doctor a little longer, as he was being tortured. He simply sat without moving—making no move to leave.

"Can you come Friday?"

"No."

"Why not?"

"Because I don't live here. I am staying 150 miles from here."

"Oh. I didn't know that. When can you come?" The doctor still felt there was some money out there somewhere to pay for this.

"I don't know. I'm not sure that I want to come back to see you."

"Why not?"

"I don't see the point."

"Well, if you want help, I'm here."

"So long."

"Good by." But then, he held out a bottle of pills to Peter. "Try some of these," he said, smiling.

"What are they?"

"Just a mild tranquillizer. Take one when you think you need to calm down." What? Peter was still at a point in his life where he fed on anger. Calm down? When he got that anger channeled into something constructive, as he invariably did, it fueled a great creativity. What ever happened to sublimation?

"What is the name of it?"

The doctor mumbled something Peter did not understand.

"I am trying to get off pills. They led to a suicide attempt once. I don't want any more chemicals in my system, and I don't want temptation around."

"These will help you. Try them. Do it for me, will you? You want us to help you, don't you?"

"I don't know that I want that kind of help."

"Have you used tranquilizers before?"

"I just said I did."

"Who gave them to you?"

"A doctor friend back East."

"Did they help you?"

Yes, for a time. Somewhat. But I want to fight this out without pills."

"Take them."

Peter took the bottle of pills and left the office, depressed. He never took the pills, of course, and threw them into the nearest garbage can.

Chapter 14

Peter went to the St. Peter and Paul Cathedral in San Francisco. It was dark inside. Not completely dark. Light came inside through the stained glass windows. It was cloudy, and not much light came into the cathedral. Many small candles flickered on both sides of the altar.

Some churches did not have votive candles. He tried to find cathedrals where there were candles, and he would drop a quarter in the offering box and light one of them, saying a short prayer. Sometimes he didn't have a quarter, so he faked it with a penny. He had to give that up too, one day.

A bent old lady put a coin into the tin box at the foot of the candles, and the sound echoed through the stone church.

It was cold inside. It was so still that a young man, saying his rosary at the other end of the church, could be heard clearly. A priest appeared out of a side door, his face old and mottled, pale. He had the self indulgent, possessive, soft look of a child molester.

The priest entered a confessional box. A very bent and tortured old man moved down the aisle. He was crippled up from arthritis, and his right leg was bent from polio. Another old man came along behind him, his skull concave from a blow, as though he'd been hit with a large, round rock.

Peter said a few prayers which he knew by heart. He always said the same ones because he didn't know any others: The Lord's Prayer, the Twenty Third Psalm, which was to him a prayer, and the Hail Mary, for which he did not know all of the words.

"Hail Mary, full of grace. Mother of God. Blessed is the fruit of thy womb, Jesus...." He said the King James version of the Twenty Third Psalm. Since it was rewritten in modern versions, it wasn't the same. The new versions lost the poetry. The King James version had great beauty, in his opinion. It was from another age.

> *The Lord is my shepherd; I shall not want.*
> *He maketh me to lie down in green pastures: he leadeth me beside the still waters.*
> *He restoreth my soul: He leadeth me in the paths of righteousness for his name's sake.*
> *Yea, though I walk through the valley of the shadow of death, I will fear no evil: for thou art with me; thy rod and thy staff they comfort me.*
> *Thou preparest a table before me in the presence of mine enemies: thou anointest my head with oil; my cup runneth over.*
> *Surely goodness and mercy shall follow me all the days of my life: and I will dwell in the house of the LORD forever.*

"Protect my mother and father," he asked. "Keep them safe, no matter what they did to me in the past." He forgave them, but then he saw that he was not forgiving those who had ruined his career. He was fighting them. What about turning the other cheek? What about forgiving those who trespassed against us? What about all that in the Church which taught political docility?

Tell that to the modern activists in the Church. He wasn't ready to turn the other cheek.

"What should I do, God?" He always asked that question, and the message always came back: "*Fight them!*" So he filed suits, and harassed his former employer. He was a thorn in their side and battled them. Someone had to. Someone had to show that they didn't take it lying down.

He had one shot at a career as a professional writer, and he either blew it, or had this terrible thing happen to him at the start. It was dashed. All ruined along with his mind.

He longed for death sometimes. He was broken hearted in that church. Tears flooded his eyes. He had suffered enough. "Enough, God!" he railed in his mind. "End it!" Peter looked at the old people in the church and saw their suffering. He saw young people come in and go to the front pews, bowing before the altar before kneeling on the cushion and praying. They were in mourning and wore black arm bands. He prayed for them.

"I want to die."

Yea, though I walk through the valley of the shadow of death, I will fear no evil: for thou art with me: thy rod and thy staff they comfort me.

"I will fear no evil because I'm the meanest son-of-a-bitch in the valley," he laughed.

Strength came to him, for a little while, in that church.

He thought of all the tragedy in the world. Millions of people suffering and starving, and wars raged. There was so much suffering.

"Have I turned the other cheek?" No.

He had a vision of Christ spilling over the money tables. Jesus was very angry when he went into the temple to do that. He was in revolt. No wonder he got what he got. Nobody liked to have pointed out to them such things as Jesus revolted against: money tables and pigeons sold in the temple.

He knew that sometimes people must fight, must revolt. Christianity must not be used as the opiate of the people to control them.

But he knew also that there was nothing so terrible as fighting and resistance, either a legal fight, or the blood of the battlefield. If there was some other way that people could treat one another. If people could treat one another *right*. Fat chance.

"Business is business," the lawyer had said. "They are in business to make money." And they have to do it at the expense of someone else.

Every system is a tyranny.

He went out on the street in the middle of North Beach with its bright sunshine, peculiarly clear air, and white light. "Can you spare a couple of pennies?" a small boy asked. Peter gave the boy a quarter.

Another asked a moment later: "Can you spare any change?" He was a young fellow, clean looking.

"No. Sorry, I'm broke too." But he wasn't. He could have given it to him, but didn't. The guy looked like an addict.

An old man in a ragged coat, tall, with a very white and curly beard a foot long—an old man that looked like death and life at the same time, with great, round, sad brown eyes, a man looking like an Old Testament prophet, yet terribly sad, on Mission Street, staring at the window of a cheap restaurant, maybe studying the prices on the printed photos of hamburgers or grilled cheese sandwiches and cokes in the windows, or looking at the food inside on the tables, or at the people eating.

Peter stopped him: "Are you hungry?" Peter asked him.

"Yes." His big sad eyes looked directly at him, unblinking.

Peter pressed a dollar bill into the old man's hand, out of guilt for turning the last man down.

"God bless you."

I need it, Peter though.

Peter walked away. The old man, slightly bent, stared after him for half a block, then turned, and walked off.

Twenty-five thousand people a year die of cold in the United States, a modern progressive country that does not look after its homeless people. But the problems of the homeless are not so easy.

Did he still believe in God? Yes, But he doubted. *"Why would you treat me like this? Why are all these people living on the streets and without their own home? Why is this terrible war and suffering going on here and there and everywhere without end? Why are little children taken from their parents and violated and killed? Why are beautiful young people killed in the prime of their life from accidents and disease?"*

Peter always was put in mind of the story of Job. Job was made to endure great suffering, as Peter was, as a test of his faith. Something kept him safe as long as he remembered to pray. As long as he remembered God—a force and power in life greater than ourselves. Peter made a mistake, though. He did not understand that he would be all right. He saw people killed, have accidents, die. He did not put his trust in God day to day. It took several more years before he learned to give thanks for each blessing as it came. He had to be reduced to the gutter before he would understand that he was *powerless*, and that his fate, the fate of all mankind, was in the hands of power far greater than anything man could do, contrary to the Catholic theory, that *we* are responsible for our fate. Catholic priests would want people to believe that we are responsible for what happens to us when so many of them were busy having sex with young children and youth. The only people responsible were the priests.

The very action of the spheres, of the Moon and the planets, the movement of the continental plates, and the speed of the Earth around the sun, the changing tilt of the Earth's axis and reversal of the Earth's magnetic field was far beyond the hand or will of man, of body time and the body's internal clock, the menses of women in tune with the fullness of the Moon, the ionic changes in the body day to day caused by weather and the wind, and so much else, those things affected us far more.

The brain is mostly water. Why should not the Moon pull on it, against the skull, and effect us in some way with this pressure as it does the any other body of water?

Once Peter had camped for several months by Frenchman's Bay across from Bar Harbor near the sea, only ten feet from the highest tide when he began his first major non-fiction work. He stayed there until the intense cold of December drove him away. After some weeks his body seemed to respond to the rhythm of the tides. He became acutely sensitive to the Moon and its phases, and to the weather. The lapping of the waves at the water's edge became a part of his body and his soul. He had so many times slept on the beach by the ocean farther south. He came into complete harmony with nature, and then for a time he had regained all that is lost from humanity in the cities, from the teeming masses with electricity from a thousand power lines throbbing through their bodies, when he expunged the chlorine from his body tissue and drank pure water, and breathed the pure air of the sea and mountains and banished the poisons of machines and factories from his lungs and body.

The planets one after another, like jewels strung on a long thread above the horizon across the sky overhead—Jupiter, Mars, and Saturn—chased each other through the Zodiac, and Venus, brilliant, running from them, catching them, until all were in line one behind the other, strung out in a straight line from the Sun, with the unseen planets: Pluto, Neptune, and Uranus, and little Mercury speeding far faster round and round the Sun until it too was in its place all in a line with the others in conjunction…Wow!

Seeing the planets all together put him in communion with people farther back in time, in pre-Columbian history, with Druids, Mayas, Teotihuacanos, Egyptians and Babylonians, with all those ancient people who lived in harmony with the cosmos in civilizations perhaps far superior to our own. Who knows?

He walked through the city.

There was a vision in a cathedral once. It was at Easter service, and there were twelve priests preparing communion for the people. There was a long table before them, and for a moment he saw the Last Supper.

For a moment—a long moment—Peter felt the back of his head tingle with that presence from outside of this world, that came down to us briefly, and he was thrust backwards two thousand years, and the bearded priests had the long flowing white linen of the disciples around them. Christ was among them.

Tears came to his eyes. He looked around him when it was safe to move, and many in the congregation had tears in their eyes. Perhaps they had seen it too. Perhaps Christ had visited them all and been among them in that church in Cambridge near Harvard Square.

Later in his life, a vision of the living Christ on the cross would come to him in his darkest hour.

Broadway in San Francisco, with scores of bars, bottomless, topless, naked women inside, lovely nude college girls dancing, looking the customers in the eyes.

"Hi! I'm Heather. Can you make a donation for the jukebox?" the girl asked, her breasts naked and saucy, pressing against his bare arm, warm, beckoning...

"You look like a student at U.C. Berkeley, Heather," he said.

"I am. That's what this place is all about: 'Co-ed topless dancers.'" She had a baby face and was a baby, looking very young. She wore little make-up and looked sixteen. It would be fun to put diapers on her. Her warm pussy pressed against the back of his hand. Peter felt that in every corner of his trembling body.

She also looked like the twin of the Moony that had hooked him on the street in Berkeley and had him coming by for dinner every day, then having secret meetings with him elsewhere, gradually revealing her doubts about what she was doing, until they took her away—not before she had given him the address of her parents and asked him to call them for her. When she suddenly disappeared that night, by luck he found out from another young Moony girl where they had taken her north of the City. There are many ways the young are hooked and put to the uses of others...Christ, how he desired that girl captured by the Moonys. The Rev. Sun Moon, a Korean entrepreneur, became very rich avoiding taxes and making a fortune from many beautiful kids whoring for him on the streets of America's university towns. Were they much different than the college girls that put in vacations and stints in Nevada where they could sell it and bank tuition quickly?

"You're very nice. Do you have some change?"

"Yes." He gave her a dollar. She went away for a moment and played some songs and came right back.

"I have to ask for money. It's my job."

"I know. I've seen it before."

"Do you spend much time in places like this?" Heather asked him.

"Not at all."

"I work here because I have to have money for school."

"I know," he said. "What are you studying?"

"That's the last question. Psychology."

"Oh." He looked at her. At her lovely breasts.

"Do you like them?"

"Yes, Heather." He breathed it.

"Do you want to touch them?"

"Yes," he said. He was so nervous it was hard to say it. He thought of her as a fragile, delicate child. So lovely. So perfect.

She took his hand and put it on her breast, on her nipples. She held it there for a moment, then took her hand away. His hand remained, hefting her breast. Then she removed it. She let his hand rest on her naked thigh. He was hurting so badly he almost passed out at the touch. It was intensely erotic to touch her in a public place like that. He was too lonely.

"You can have me for fifty dollars."

"I'd like to. I need it. I don't have the money." He stuttered.

"Can you buy me a drink? I'd like to sit with you for a moment. They watch me. I have to produce. You understand...." The bar tender hovered close, listening, watching. He was a big thug.

Peter bought her a drink, which cost three bucks. He needed the money, but he needed the closeness of a naked woman's body more. Without intimacy, a man dies inside.

Without warning, she squeezed his prick through his jeans. "I'd like to suck that," she said. She kept her hand there and felt him grow very hard.

"I'd like you to," he said. "You're very nice. Maybe I can get some money. Will you be here tomorrow night?" He was already in love with her.

"No. Next week."

"I can't stay in the City that long." He paused. "You break my heart."

"Why?"

"You're so lovely. You are truly beautiful."

"They all say that! I'm really a lot tougher than I look."

"But it's true!" And to him, she was utterly beautiful. He couldn't understand a girl that pretty working in such a dive.

The girl dancing had on Ben Franklin glasses, several tatoos, and chewed gum. She had long black hair, and her body was devoid of sensuality. Her skin had the sallow look of a heavy smoker. She had taken everything off. She just bumped and ground without feeling. When she had finished her numbers, a pretty blond, with a red bush, got up and danced. "Now, ladies and gentleman," the master of ceremonies announced, "We have pretty Michelle on the center stage. Lets hear it for Michelle!" and a few people clapped along with the M.C. "Michelle is a student at San Francisco State College...!" And there was a bit more applause.

Michelle was sensuous, her body full and erotic. Women's smell was in the place. Heather kept her hand on his prick. She was a lovely girl, but he detected a hard edge. For one so young, it had started early. The girl on the stage behind the bar lay down on her rug and spread her legs in front of them, and played with herself. Peter watched the way Heather stared at the girl offering herself to the audience, licking her lips from time to time, looking at her hungrily.

Michelle did it for another girl who sat avidly at the bar, watching everything. She did if for all the girls, for those who wanted to watch her masturbate. The blonde, good looking, got up and turned her back to them, and then bent over, separated her cheeks, and for a long time, showed her pretty anus to them, opening and closing it, and sticking her finger in it, and masturbating her clit with her other hand.

She had a beautiful ass.

"I was fucking when I was ten," Heather said. "My mother was a doctor and my father died young. Then my mother died, and there wasn't any money left. I'm obsessed with sex. Maybe it's a way of getting love. Does that answer your question?"

"I didn't ask."

"That was what you wanted to know—what is a nice girl like me doing working in a dump like this?"

"Yes. I wondered."

Another good looking young girl came up to Heather and put her arm around her, kissed her, standing hip to hip side by side and slipped her hand inside Heather's panties and clutched and fondled her pussy. Both smiled at him as he could see their fingers working each other. Heather squeezed and kissed the girl's breasts, her eyes half closed as the other's fingers got deeper inside. They tongue kissed passionately for some time.

Peter was transported. This was a dream that had often obsessed him.

"I have to go now," she said and moved on to a customer who had just sat down nearby. Her hand left his dick, and very briefly, in a flash, she kissed him. He fantasized, as he finished his beer, living with her, marrying her, worshipping her. Then he left the bar. He would never see her again, forever losing her with the ten thousand other lovely women that passed through a young man's life on the road never to be seen again. Haunting them forever with desire.

Skin flick houses everywhere in North Beach, the Tenderloin, along Market and Mission Streets. Dirty bookstores and porno movies in the stripper bars. Total eroticism (hard action) for sale. X-rated movies in the motels on Cable. Many street walkers hustling. Intelligent college girls selling their asses, prostituting themselves. Many of them just taking a course or two, keeping up the pretense or bettering themselves. "Want a date, honey?"

If he'd had the money, he would have rented one of the pretty college girls. He never had the money.

Gays and transvestites flooding the streets. Huge, tough black men dressed in women's clothes and heavy make up with exaggerated false eyelashes, toddling along on high heals and shaved legs in hose, uglier than shit.

Coffee houses and countless bars.

He saw one of the FBI men go into an S & M movie with a black bus driver in uniform. Hard trade, he thought.

They all had their own sickness, their own secret lives. Peter was no more weird than any other.

He walked into a dozen bars and another dozen, thinking about Heather. She was still in his mind and would be for a few hours or a couple of days. Or until the next girl....

He walked into another bar and a gorgeous young blonde was right beside the door, in a human size bird cage, absolutely naked. She smiled at him. "Come right on in!" she said. But he turned and went out, after devouring her fifteen year old body with his eyes. She had a fake I.D. to work there. He smiled at her. How many went to such places thinking of their daughters? Or to *see* them....

Her pudendum was inches from his face. He stared at it, and the delicate hair, like down. It hypnotised him. It was so close....

"Do you like my pussy?"

"Yes."

"Stay. Buy me a drink when I get out of the cage."

"I'll come back," he said, still staring. The need to reach out and touch, to kiss and lick was overwhelming. He had to run away or die. He was afraid....

"That's what they all say," she said, smiling, disappointed.

Overwhelming loneliness for a woman grabbed him.

Then there was the live action sex on the stage—beautiful young lesbians dancing and stripping together, caressing each other, holding each other's breasts, eating each other out.

He had become so depressed that he took one of the pills the doctor gave him, no longer caring about anything. They reacted badly with the drinks. Nobody said anything about that.

In another bar there were dark booths raised above the floor. A beautiful waitress, naked, lead him to a table and he bought a two dollar half-bottle of beer, smelling her perfume, past girls blowing, sucking, licking, jerking off men in the darkness of the booths. He wanted to go back and see the blond in the last bar. Why did he run? Was he so afraid that she was the dream he had been chasing and that he had found her in such a place? She was the fantasy he chased, for sure.

"You want to fuck in the back room?" The waitress said, after studying his hips and his body.

"No. I haven't got money with me." He didn't have it at all. And, he'd always been reluctant to go for it.

He downed the beer quickly, not liking the girl who was dancing on the stage, and left the bar and went to a coffee shop in North Beach and tried to pick up a girl. There was one, sitting alone in a lovely dress, drinking a capuchino and smoking a long filter cigarette. He smiled big, "Boy, that's a beautiful dress...."

"Don't bother me," she said very quick and very tough. "I don't want to be hit on."

Soon, his thoughts turned back to the young blonde in the cage. His heart ached.

He missed his friends in the East and thought about going back. There wasn't much sense in staying in California any longer. He wasn't relating to it, and things had gone too badly. He was used to the tension of the East, the social pressure cooker that drove him on to achieve and grow, to learn and create.

But he knew there was nothing there for him, either. He had somehow to hang on and persevere, if he was ever going to amount to anything.

He did those things in California. He wrote. But he was too alone there. Life was too much on the surface. The seamy undercurrents were ugly, and there was not much depth to anything. The women were poisoned against men and life after they were twenty. It was like being dragged along the bottom beneath the breakers on the beach. He felt like he was drowning.

Peter had many friends. But he had been put on the run, and had got too far away. He had been conned into going out West on this trip, severing him from the ties and friendships that he needed. This wasn't his home. What the hell was he doing in California? He came up short, with a start. But, he had all but started his life in California as a child.

"What the hell am I doing out here?" He was so exposed and vulnerable, that somebody might kill him and nobody would give it a second thought. It would merely be the death of another vagrant, not worthy of mention in the morning newspaper.

Boy, had he been had! Sent out there on a wild goose chase by a publisher on speculation—that never paid him a cent or helped make the project work. What a fool he was! They had just wanted to get rid of him.

While walking, he ran into an attractive girl he vaguely knew, and was invited to a party. Peter was full of valium and booze. All he could think about was the naked girl in the cage. The girl who invited him was mildly attractive, but she wore so many astrological symbols that she was in outer space searching for a Taurus.

There was something else about her, too. It was as though she had been dehumanized. The girl radiated sex and hooked on the street now and then. She had a regular job, but she seemed very cold beneath a pleasant exterior. She used sex and her body to turn people on, but it went no-where. He knew. He had tried.

He noticed the pentagram hanging from her neck. But it did not connect in his mind. He did not realize what she was.

She lived a double life.

The house belonged to a doctor. The doctor looked at him lasciviously, perhaps with homosexual desire, when Peter came in. The doctor was making some joints for everyone. He wore a beard like that of the devil. He also wore a thick metal pentagram around his neck.

Peter tried to smoke a little dope that night. Grass never had done much of anything for him, so he avoided it. Sometimes it was impossible to avoid. He couldn't inhale it anyway.

Peter took three drags on the joint as it was passed around, and then he couldn't breathe. He felt as though he was dying.

"I can't breathe," he said.

"Good dope, huh?"

"You are a doctor?"

"Yes."

"What is your specialty?"

"I'm a psychiatrist."

"Oh, really?"

"Well, I don't practice anymore.

"What do you do?"

"I help…people…who need help…" He was holding his breath full of dope as he spoke a word at a time.

"The Human Potential Movement?"

"Yes."

"Does the government pay for that? Do they pay you money?"

"Yes.

"I need help. I can't breathe. What's in the dope?"

"That's your own trip! *That's your own trip!*" He shouted, suddenly like a mad man. "You're smoking it. You took responsibility!" Something was going radically wrong with this guy very fast. His tone was insistent, changed, panicked, deranged. Perverse. Sick. Something was going radically wrong with Peter equally as fast.

"I think I'm having a bad reaction. I can't breathe right. My breathing and my heartbeat are out of synchronization. I'm dizzy. I'm frightened," he said with clinical detachment.

"You are *all right*," the girl said. She was a person without a name, without an identity, almost without a face.

"Don't *deprive* him. Don't *deprive* him," the crazy doctor with the beard like the devil's said.

"Can someone get me to a hospital?"

"Don't *deprive* him," the doctor said.

Everything went around. He tried to use the asthma inhalator to try to get more air, but couldn't inhale.

The girl had hold of his arm and pinched him so roughly that he went with her as she took him out the door. She was operating on instinct, against her program. She saved him.

The girl took him to the hospital. He fell down on the floor, and they let him lie there. "He puts ibocaine in it," she told him. "He experiments on us. We let him because he takes care of us."

He lay on the floor, very frightened. Everything went around.

His heart beat in a wild arrhythmia. He had a dangerous asthmatic attack and could not expel the air from his lungs.

A death chill stole over him. His heart was out of phase. Tachycardia or arrhythmia, he did not know. He knew that he had little pulse. He had used the Bronchometer to control the bronchospasm, but the medicine compounded things. It caused depression and tension. Wasn't there a better medicine?

He felt several times that he was going to die, as he lay there. He knew that he was facing death. The girl had left. "I have to get back," she said. Get back to what?

"He's a psychiatric case," a doctor told the girl. She left. They simply let him lie on the floor.

"If you don't get up and get out of here, we'll call the police," an administrative employee said to him. He didn't have any medical insurance. Maybe that was it. They didn't want him to die on their doorstep. He did not know how lucky he was the girl got him out of the doctor's house. He might never have got out alive. But, he started to breath a little better.

For a little while he talked. Things came out in a flood. "They are trying to kill me," he said. He was manic, speaking fast. Then suddenly his strength left him and he collapsed again. They gave him a heavy shot of valium on top of the liquor in his system. His heart went wild. The combination might have killed anybody else. Valium was all the rage.

He lay there, his eyes staring off into space. He was helpless. He had to get out of there before the hospital killed him. Had they been warned in advance? He had a memory of all those asthmatics found dead with inhalators in their hand. That was what was happening to him. He tried to tell them, but failed.

His lungs were full of fluid. He had been living outdoors too long.

Peter was laid out on the floor of the waiting room in the emergency area for a long time, until two in the morning. He tried to get up. He was losing his body temperature again. Hypothermia. He hit his head when he fell down, trying to get up.

"You either leave, or we'll send you to a state hospital."

"No."

"Then we'll call the police."

"Is this a hospital?"

"Yes."

Is this America?

He was afraid. He got to the lobby and collapsed again. His heart started to fade again, but a nurse helped him. No doctor would touch him. *"Heh, this guy's got no pulse!"*

"He's faking it."

"Get him out of here. We don't want him dying in here."

"The police are coming." And they came. His heart started working again.

"Please, nurse, help me out of here." She held his hand.

"I'll be right back," she said, and went away. The police came, and were called to the other end of the room. They told the police: "The guy is on some kind of drugs. We don't want him here. He may be violent. Take him to a state hospital."

Peter slipped out of the door, barely walking. The cool air revived him a little. There was a phone booth close by and he called a friend and plead with him: "Please come and get me," he said. "Peter, we can't help you all the time. First it's money or a meal, then you need rides."

"Please. I'm real sick. They might put me in jail. They don't understand. Somebody drugged me."

"Do you take drugs?" The negotiation for the ride continued.

"No! Never! Please help me."

"We can't have you sick here."

"I just need to sleep on your couch. Just tonight. I promise."

"If we come, don't do this again. Is that understood?"

His friends came and picked him up and took him to their apartment. He threw up in the bathroom right away. He lay down, and was calm.

Peter did not sleep at all that night. He piled on many blankets and was fully dressed in bed. After awhile the death chill left, and he warmed up. He took off his clothes and some of the blankets.

At 4:45 AM he began to get rales in his chest, and then a serious bronchospasm started with lightning speed. He used the Bronchometer again, and the spasms stopped before it would have been impossible to inhale the medicine. But then his heart got out of rhythm again, and terrified him. He took more valium.

"Shouldn't be medicating myself," he said aloud. "I should be in a hospital." Two times before his heart stopped in emergency wards when they had accidentally overdosed him. Nothing was safe.

He opened the window, burning with heat. He needed to take a shit, but was afraid of passing out. He was dehydrated. He drank as much water as he could get in. His body burned up with heat.

At five in the morning he was able to take a shit without passing out, and felt better. He prayed for daylight, believing that if the light came, he would survive.

Peter remembered the face of his roommate, John Horner, in death, at the funeral home in his coffin, when he had died in agony from an overdose.

Peter knew that he might die, that his heart might give out from the strain. Ibocaine. What was that? Later he found out that it is a deadly poison in larger quantities. From Nigeria. It took very little to kill.

This had happened before in Cambridge. The exact same thing, when the trouble started with his first publisher. He'd lain on the floor of the emergency room at the Cambridge City Hospital, and they would not help him. His pulse was thready there too.

He had been drugged when he was in the mountains, sitting by the fire with a number of other campers late at night. They had put something in his tea, and in the joint they shared. He could not breathe, and there was no possibility of getting to a hospital with a one day walk to get to the road. And again as a sailor in a foreign port. More than once. And other times.

Drugging people was an old business.

It was out of Céline, the things that were happening to him. *Death On The Installment Plan.* Louis Ferdinand Céline, one of the greatest writers who ever lived.

He had a great deal of trouble with his heart, and time after time rushed to one emergency ward or another. He had fallen down in the street when they said, "*You will never be published again. We can play pretty rough.*" The bitter years passed since then and still it did not get better, the terrible words and threat did not leave his mind.

Nothing had been right since. Everything that could go wrong did. His life was ruined. He crawled from gutter to gutter.

They had psychically murdered him. It was the infliction of extreme mental anguish.

Perhaps it was a test of his faith and he failed it. He prayed hard when he knew that he faced death, and it happened more than once, but he was not ready to die, and yet, fatalistically, prepared for it. He did not accept the will of God. Each day would take care of itself, but not until he had conquered fear and panic, and melded himself into the rhythm of those forces far larger than himself.

Is it not the duty of every young person to rebel? Is it not imprinted in the genes?

Chapter 15

The small presses were challenging the power of the major publishers in the book industry in a significant way, or so they would have liked to think. They were developing their own means of distribution, and they had to be stamped out. The book industry was centralized, and more easily controlled.

Peter began to try to break out in the open.

A printer in Fort Bragg was willing to help him start a small press on credit. The printer knew it was unlikely he would get his money back anytime soon, but he took a chance, wanting to help Peter. Phil Sharples and his wife had hearts of gold.[1]

Peter was able to produce his first book as a publisher, and in the process learned how a book is made from start to finish. He was no longer just a writer but a *publisher*.

This put him on the Watch List again, or some more.

As soon as he had the book hot off the press, he took a car load to a distributer that accepted it, and signed up to exhibit his handiwork in book fairs, got interviewed on local radio stations, and lectured for free or for money taken up in a collection. If they would not publish him, he would speak out somehow, and get himself known.

---

1. Sixteen years later the Sharples got their money back when Peter hit it lucky.

But his controllers were right there, sitting on him. They were always there either in the background, or behind the scenes.

Peter was accepted at an exhibit in Berkeley. The woman in Carmel who had attached herself to him, "Lady Jane," insisted on going with him to Berkeley. He was getting tired of her, but was trying to sort out who she was and what her game was. She was far from being a lady and was run by some of the manifold retired Right Wing military and intel officers living in Carmel.

Jane talked so much on the way up to San Francisco that he kept speeding up the car and exceeding the speed limit out of anger at her, without realizing that he was doing it. She made him mad. Several times the California Highway Patrol drew up behind him out of nowhere, but he managed to see them quickly enough and slow down. She was trying to get him a ticket for speeding but he was too dumb to see it.

"*Shut up!*" he finally told her. He disliked her anyway, but she was at least there, someone in the echoing emptiness of his nightmare who listened to his demented stories. If his mind wasn't snapping at every turn from the stress he was under, he would have never spoken to her, repelled by her, but he hoped that she might—somehow—help him, and she held out that false hope. There was no way of knowing then that she had a connection with the Secret Service. He never should have exposed himself to her.

"Nixon is a dangerous man," he said. "I believe his henchmen had something to do with killing President Kennedy. And Ford covered it up!"

Congressman Gerald Ford, later President Ford, had been on the Warren Commission, and later pardoned Nixon. But Ford had settled in Rancho Mirage, California, near Frank Sinatra and so many others who had made their killing in film and entertainment. The disgraced former vice president Spiro "Spiral" Agnew was with them as well. In Palm Springs and Rancho Mirage they lived in walled fortresses, otherwise known as a "gated community," near what they had come to think of as a dangerous foreign country which spilled over its hundreds of thousands of illegal aliens who preyed upon those rich and famous who had thought they were safe out in the middle of nowhere in the desert. After all, politics is Show Business too. Many employed illegal aliens in their houses for cheap labor.

And Nixon was not far away in Southern California until he moved back to New York for some strange reason. California with all its power, closed ranks around those corrupted politicians who fed on their soul, having no other heroes but movie stars to worship.

"Fletcher Prouty wrote in *The Secret Team* that we should see what kind of jobs certain people moved into after the assassination, and then we would know what really happened."

"You believe that Ford had something to do with it?" Jane asked.

"I don't know. I know that he helped cover it up, and that he was known as the CIA's man in the House of Representatives."

Much later, to his shock, he saw a picture of her with Ford. Evil smelling she was. Her juices—if she ever had any—had long dried up. Her body abused and misshapen.

"Do you have a place to stay in Berkeley?" he had asked before he took her with him. "Yes," she said. But she lied.

His nerves were frayed from the drive with Jane from Carmel to Berkeley. He was wrung out when he got there.

He set up his exhibit at the book fair in Berkeley, which was being held at a school. Jane glued herself to him every moment. She talked incessantly. As always, he was nice to her. "Get lost" he should have said. She sat down at his exhibit and proceeded to talk him to death, scaring people off who wanted to ask questions or talk. She took careful note of whomever he might know—who his contacts were. She harassed him the whole day, questioned him, wearing him out, running him down. She brought over flakes of all kinds to further tax him. Jane never went away. She was currying favor with someone. Many impecunious women curried favor sucking up with the authorities, with political people, with the socially connected to get some leverage. These self appointed informers were the raw material of countless second rate information networks.

"Don't you have something else to do?" He finally asked her.

"No."

"I thought you had people to see in town."

"No."
"Where are you going to stay?"
"I don't know."
"Well, there's a cheap hotel on Bankcroft Avenue."
"I don't want to stay there."
"Why not?"
"I don't have the money."
"Come on Jane, you can't be that broke!" He was angry, exasperated.
"No. I don't know where I'm going to stay." She knew he was a soft touch, if he had it. He always tried to help people. That was how she was going to stick with him like glue.
"But you told me you were going to.... that you had a place to stay."
"No, *I didn't*. You misunderstood me. I didn't hear you right—are we going to stay here two days?"
"I am. The fair lasts two days," Peter said.
"Where are you going to stay?"
"Here," he said.
"Here?"
"Yes."
"I don't understand," she said.
"Exhibiters can sleep on the floor here. I brought a sleeping bag."
"Can I stay here as well?"
"I suppose so." It was ludicrous. Now he had her to worry about and take care of.

Peter ended up giving her his sleeping bag and his pillow, and she stayed there over night, never leaving him alone, never letting him talk to other people.

"I thought you were going to take some pictures of the Fair," he said.

"I don't have any film for my camera." Was he supposed to buy it for her?

The game was to be as much of a problem for him as possible.

He hated her. What a fool he was. She had already caused him so much trouble, and the consequences would be a lot more trouble the following winter.

In the end, *they* threw all they had at him, but were unable to bring him down. The more they tried, the harder he fought. He matured on this anvil. Like molten metal, he was being tempered. Had they gotten more overt with their provocations, then he might have gone into open revolt. They could have shot him down. It was all but impossible to successfully revolt in an organized nation-state where oppression was far too subtle, where *stability* over a hundred years—with riots, depressions and so on— had entrenched the military power of the exploiters.

During his long hikes he studied and absorbed the forests and mountains and regenerated, and regained his strength and perspective.

He believed that the perseverance of lone individuals, fighting alone, with no groups behind them, might be able to effect change. It was a crazy idea but worth a try. He always believed that one nut like him could throw a monkey wrench into any rotten system and make so much noise about it that he could change it. Change the way people think. Then, in time, the groups, like the trendy lemmings they were, would fall in step with those who march to a distant drummer. There were many examples of such lone sentinel pines changing things.

Like Rosa Parks who sat down in the front of a bus when she was supposed to sit in the back when black people had to do that years ago in Montgomery, Alabama, and the rest of the South, and wouldn't get up and move. A great movement started because of her simple act, and the entire behavior of a ruthless racist nation was changed.

There are many examples.

After the Berkeley exhibition, Peter entered the huge San Francisco book fair that year. He got ready. While Peter waited for the fair, he camped out on the coast. A letter came from a lady he did not know, in Carmel, asking that they meet. She had heard about him from a lecture he'd given, and from a piece in the paper. He called her and went over for a visit.

She was a gracious, aristocratic lady, growing old. It appeared that she did not quite have enough money in her retirement. She talked about not having enough quite a lot, like she wanted him to give her some. She had worked for Time & Life for many years. He became certain that someone had asked the lady to contact him.

They talked quite awhile. "Why don't you try to get a job teaching?" she suggested.

"Oh, I am looking. Jobs are hard to find."

"Why don't you think about *Canada*. There might be some jobs teaching there. Why not try Saskatchewan? Or, write to the University of Alberta."

"That's rather far from here, don't you think?"

"So many bad things have happened to you in this country. Wouldn't you want to leave? Wouldn't it be better somewhere else? I mean, you have had so much bad luck here and hate it so!"

"I don't hate it."

"Well, it certainly sounds like you do. You criticize it all the time."

"Is that not allowed? Are we not allowed to point out problems?"

"Well, I don't think those are problems. It is still the best country in the world!"

Love it or leave it.

"I feel that would be deserting my country. There is a fight to be fought here for the future. If that fight is lost, if this country goes down, then they all go down," Peter said. "I am not going to run away. I have run away before. Beside, Saskatchewan is awfully far away. I have run far enough in this life, and it's time to stop. That would be like going to Siberia, wouldn't it? Wouldn't I be in exile there? I've got to fight this thing out directly. There's no going off to the woods and hiding anymore."

Then she came out in the open: "Why don't you call off your fight with that publisher? You can't fight City Hall. You can't win against them. They have the largest law firms and great power and this just costs everybody a lot of money. You can't beat them and you don't want them against you."

He looked at her, taken aback. Had she been talking to them? Did they ask her to say this? "They are already against me. I haven't done anything wrong. They have smashed my life because I could not do what they asked me to do." The awful pain struck him like a sledge hammer.

She paused for a moment. "You are exhibiting in San Francisco, aren't you, at the book fair?"

"Yes."

"I'd like to visit you there."

"Sure."

Peter heard from one of his professors, whose letter was very strange: "I received your letter of the 26th. Understand your feelings. Weather at the present is extremely changeable. Very warm some days; extremely cold on others. This has made gardening very hard. I have had to replace a lot of things I had started myself.

"I have some registered mail waiting for me in Boston. I have been away. Will advise on fall weather forecast.

"Sorry to be so vague, but this letter might be opened and read by someone else." This was a signal for Peter to call him from a safe telephone. His professor told him: "Anybody who knows anything about Kennedy's death is being watched. The things that are happening to you are happening because of the Kennedy case. The murder was political..."

He had been one of Kennedy's teachers.

When Peter resumed trips to Dallas to investigate what he could, he was afraid. There was the time that he spent awake the entire night lying on a couch while an employee of Parkland hospital sat in the kitchen with a loaded revolver on the table.

"There is no law," his friend said. "There is no *justice*. There is only law and justice for those who can afford it. The more money and power you have, the more law and justice you get. The poor get nothing, only a show." Years of painful study in law school didn't teach that. "It's a police state," his friend insisted.

People were being killed up and down the beaches of California as they slept in their sleeping bags.

Someone was found hanging from a tree in Sausalito.

Young girls were abducted from the streets and even their homes and from slumber parties, raped and killed, thrown out of cars dead, or dumped in the woods. Three hundred children a year were snatched off the streets by total strangers.

There were earthquakes and the ground shook.

The book fair lasted three days. Peter set up his exhibit early the first morning, and the lady who wanted him to go to Saskatchewan came before the place was even opened. She sat with him for three hours, but did not disrupt him as Jane had. She just watched.

The techniques of destabilization and harassment were relentless. Time after time he was sucked in by people who befriended him, whom he thought were friends, and who then betrayed him. Peter turned the other cheek again and again, and refused to face how people betrayed him. They were told that he was a potentially dangerous radical, or anything at all, and every opening they found with him, every vulnerable point, they stuck a knife in, and tried to get him into trouble.

They tried to wear him down, watch him, and find out who his friends and contacts were.

There were two or three hundred exhibits. The Fair was held at the Presidio, an army base in San Francisco. That was a good place to watch the radicals and intellectuals, and keep the crowds away. The book fair was sabotaged from the start by a provocateur employed by one of the distributors used by the small presses.

The big publishers from the East had planted their spies and saboteurs in the action in California, while pushing the distributors out West to take their books.

The provocateur who tried to ruin the Fair was shortly paid back by a major publisher, and hired in New York. He had got their line of occult and mystical books laid on all those flakes in California.

The provocateur hired a rock band with what seemed like the biggest amplifiers and speakers ever heard in San Francisco. They were so loud that the noise carried for several miles, and police and MP's finally threatened to close down the fair. Instead, our provocateur held fast until there was action against him.

This same provocateur had sabotaged the distribution of Peter's book when he was setting up his small press.

The exhibitors were a bookish sort, artistic and intellectual people who lived quiet, impoverished, introspective lives. There were several hundred present in the huge room, proudly displaying books of poetry often lovingly printed on fine paper, sometimes handmade, illustrated, sometimes printed with hand set type a page at a time. To many the art of book-making was a craft, an end in itself. Here were many small presses that were the nucleus of a new industry that might someday destroy the power of the big centralized and secretly government controlled and led publishers and distributors—that is, if they could solve the marketing problems. These were the days when they were still shaking in their boots from the Kennedys.

Big publishers had to keep things under control.

No one could hear anyone speak. Visitors were blasted out of the area, out of the building by the terrible noise of the monkeys with their electronic toys. Peter could not think. Pain showed on everyone's face. No one could talk. Peter could feel the ultra-sonic and sub-sonic frequencies beamed at them from the electronic machinery, controlling their emotions. The enormous output of decibels threatened to start an earthquake.

Stupid New Age women stood close to the speakers nursing newborn babies or with their small children, smiling dumbly, smoking a joint, swaying and undulating with the music in their long skirts, tie dye shirts and beads. The bathrooms were filled with people shooting up heroin and snorting lines of coke. The smell of marijuana was everywhere. Sometimes Peter engaged in tough arguments with the women he saw keeping their children and babies near speakers at "concerts" who forever ruined the delicate and still unformed hearing of those babies.

The violence of American contemporary popular music intruded and destroyed the mood at the fair, driving out visitors. That was the idea.

Peter reached his breaking point, half mad anyway and with no stress tolerance at all. He spoke to the provocateur who hired the band and tried to get him to close them down, but failed. After all, who was Peter to tell him to stop it?! Then Peter went to the bandstand and threw a jumbo four foot tall plastic garbage can at the speakers, knocking one set over. He shouted at them, "***Get out of here! Get the hell out of here, you sons-of-bitches!***"

Peter then retreated into the depths of the exhibiting hall and sat at the table behind his books, trembling. Some women and poets, some exhibiters came over and thanked him. The hard rock "music" stopped, crashingly. The silence was unbelievable. People's bodies continued to vibrate and tremble with the terrible decibel assault of the barrage of sonic waves that had been attacking them. The very walls still held that vibration and the abortion of nature. Finally, even the building quieted down, and so did everyone. Slowly.

It took awhile for the band to find him, because Peter had run back to his table. They marched up and surrounded him threateningly, ready to fight, their long hair flying, their eyes glaring hate and rage, their cheeks flushed with anger and drugs, their armpits stinking of sweat and filth. Some intellectual atmosphere, that book fair.

"Did you throw that can at us?"

"No."

"We saw you do it."

"You were pointed out to us as having done it."

"Then why ask me if I did it, jerk?" He was trembling and afraid. Having to take responsibility and the consequences for his own impulsive interventions in shit was never the easiest thing in the world.

"What did you do that for?"

"I don't like the kind of noise you were making. I hate it. This is not the place for it."

"Everyone else likes it very much!" their leader spit out with great venom. How did he know?

"Many people hate it. It's just a trend. It will be gone soon. You'll be out of a job. Back to digging ditches."

"Wise guy! We were hired to perform here. This is a *concert*. You can't interfere with *artists*, God damn you!"

"Listen, shit-for-brains, *we* are the artists. This book fair is an intellectual event. You are no more an artist than an aardvark. The asshole who hired you made a stupid mistake. We should have had chamber music, if music was needed."

"Chamber music?"

"I know, you don't know what it is."

"What is it?" their female vocalist asked. Her bare nipples protruded strongly through her tee shirt, which Peter wasn't too busy not to notice.

"Don't talk to him!" Their leader said, slapping her angrily. "You don't have to talk to him. You don't need to know that. He's nothing. He's *dirt*." A few spectators began to gather around.

"Get out of here!" Peter ordered.

"Heh!" She rubbed her face, and tears sprang to her eyes.

"Step outside with us."

"Why?"

"We want to talk to you."

"I don't need to go outside to talk to you."

"Why did you throw that can at us? That is violence. We are against violence. Haven't you learned anything?" the band leader shouted.

"I didn't throw that can at you. You have the wrong guy. But we all don't like the noise you were making. Everybody has been complaining." The last statement was absolutely accurate. Naturally, nobody was going to do anything about it, though. It took a passionate garbage can thrower to do it, something like hurling a javelin.

"We *saw* you throw it at us."

"Come on you filthy liar! Come on outside!" and the pig grabbed Peter's shirt and tried to drag him away. Peter went down to the floor in a demonstration of non violence.

"I threw it at your speakers, not at you. There is a distinction." Peter was able, therefore, to plausibly deny everything, and was becoming a secret agent. He got to his feet and held down his chair again with his lead ass.

The provocateur and saboteur (we are indebted to the French for so many succinct contributions to our language such as the aforesaid descriptive phrases) who had hired the band and helped organize the fair came over. "*You'll have to leave now. We're closing down your exhibit.*"

"I'm not leaving, asshole. It doesn't work that way. It's you that is going to leave," Peter replied, stalling, calmly. Hurt in his heart. Many people gathered around.

"Do you want me to call the police?"

"Go ahead. Call them." There it was. The *police*. He was a dangerous character, and violent, too. A trouble-maker, soon to be a trespasser. Peter was scared. Deeply hurt now. His cheeks were red hot. His vision restricted.

He knew that he had some silent rooters there. Why didn't they say anything? He had to go it alone. Why him? He was past caring what they did to him. The important thing, always, was to take a stand.

He opened his big mouth before and since many times. He would never change, and many times he paid for it, developing a reputation. He was his own worst enemy, too. The guy couldn't keep quiet!

There was so much trouble everywhere he went. Tears would have come to his eyes had they all not been around him like that, inspecting him and glaring at him, as though he were an insect, or a violent hostile beast to be hurled down and snuffed out, not a sensitive man appalled by the barbarity and insensitivity of the half civilized world around him, of a society reduced to the lowest common denominator by pop culture, so to speak. The crowd needed gladiators and circuses. They needed to observe conflict close up, so that they might learn more than what TV football and cop shows showed them. True conflict was being expunged from a drugged, tuned out nation.

"*Pack up and get out!*"

"Yeah, come on outside. We want to talk to you."

Other exhibitors came over. A large crowd had gathered.

"The music was too loud," a lady said to the saboteur.

"He shouldn't have thrown that can at them."

"I would have done the same thing," the lady said. "I didn't have the nerve he had. We all would have done the same thing. That noise was all wrong for this fair and destroyed everything. We couldn't hear ourselves think, we could no longer function at all. Let him stay. We don't want any music!" She was real mad, and Peter perked up. He was grateful. He had friends. It often happened when he spoke for others that it was usually for the majority. He just didn't bother to ask before he reacted or acted for what was right. It was just that there was always a price to pay!

Then the police came, and it didn't happen the way they thought it would happen. The *government* of the City of San Francisco and the U.S. Army at the Presidio was disturbed by the noise. In fact a large part of The City was. The military authorities at the Fort were disturbed. Everyone was disturbed, even some people over in Berserkeley were disturbed when the wind was right. Everyone was disturbed, but no one at the fair was disturbed enough to act. Beside, the people at the fair were *paralyzed* from the noise. No one *thinks* to question the noise pollution we live with deliberately forced on us to string us out, distract us, and smash the private life of the mind essential to true freedom! (Authors are permitted 1-2 speeches when writing a new book. This is one of them.)

"Intellectuals lack the capacity to take strong action and are cowards," his friend Jonathan pontificated the next night over a beer. "That's the whole point of an educational system based on conditioning and exterior direction: to drive out women and men of action, and to promote the weakest and most mentally shallow. It's the natural direction of an egalitarian society to level everything to the lowest common denominator, which is Pop Culture. It's the *Leveling Process*. They are going to get us all down to their level.

"This is why 'intellectuals' are scorned, because only nitwits can get promoted into positions of power. Anyone with a real brain is too much of a threat to be allowed to get anywhere in the modern nation-state."

Jonathan was always like that. Long winded and highfalutin.

"It's all bull shit," Peter replied profoundly, wallowing in his beer. "It's all crap."

People are conditioned to screening out background harassments, loud "music", and noise pollution, while somehow trying desperately to cope. Who wants to stick their neck out?

So Peter was allowed to stay, and of course, the worst happened. A talk-radio host went around interviewing people for an NPR show, and out of 200 or 300 exhibitors, he paused longest with Peter, who laid a spectacularly articulate rap on him, being quite hung over and prone to such indulgences in that condition, and desperate as he was to assert himself and recover some sense of identity, with all of his accumulated bitterness and anger channeled into an analysis of the book business, and, of course, the assassination of the President. After all, he had been to a good school. Beside, the radio host had seen him throw the can the day before. Peter did not stand on false dignity. In fact, he had no dignity at all.

"Would you appear on my radio show Sunday night?"

"How long is it?"

"Two hours. I'll interview you."

"Okay."

Well, the CIA (everybody's favorite scapegoat and whipping boy, but it could have been somebody that looked like the CIA. After all, no-one else at the book fair had a suit and tie on) didn't like that one bit. They had a man standing right there, listening to the conversation at Peter's table, and they tried to stop the broadcast. Of course the man was operating on his own. He didn't have to consult the Company for instructions. That was the trouble with them. The whole thing was a rogue elephant.

"Who do you think killed the President?"

"It was an amalgam of Texas oil men, banking interests, rogue intelligence agents, military men, J. Edgar Hoover, and Lyndon Johnson."

"Did you leave anybody out?"

"I don't think so."

Peter had a poster up at his table about his last lecture on the assassination at a small college in Arcata. Two creeps from the CIA appeared. One of them said his name was Donald Rome, and he was vaguely foreign. Cuban, maybe. They took a photograph of Peter before he could stop them. They listened to the long talk with the radio show personality, and interrupted it frequently. They heard it all. All the details. They knew where the broadcast was going to be.

"Don't put that guy on the radio. He's unstable, and you don't want the kind of trouble that comes with this…"

There was a moment's rest, a moment of respite that night. A young lady who had manned the switchboard at the Fort and taken all the complaints about the hard rock noise from the police and the populace, sought him out and took our brave hero home to bed with her—thus providing a gentle reward. He would have slept with any girl that walked that night. Well, actually, he did that normally, when he could get it.

How she found him he wasn't sure, but he *was* a bit of a hero in some quarters, though certain he was that his distributor would stop distributing his book altogether and the printer would lose his money. A hard working couple in Fort Bragg at Mendocino Printers took a chance on him. They waited a long time for their money. Years. But they got it.

He was very grateful to that girl, whose name slipped away.

Sunday was the final day of the Fair, which generally turned out a success. That night he drove to the radio station across the Bay Bridge to Oakland. Calls came into the station right up to the very last moment, as they tried to stop the broadcast, and men with walkie-talkies stood outside in the darkened doorways across the street, watching.

"Don't put him on. He's unstable. He might say or do anything. He's trouble, that guy!"

But they put him on, and Peter told it like it was. He said anything he wanted to say for two hours. The host treated him with respect from the start. From that moment in those tough days, he began to find his metier.

The secret agents of industry didn't like that. Not one bit.

"Get ready to duck!" Donald Rome told him over the phone, just before he began to speak on the radio.

"Get ready to duck!" And, it was true. You make a move, and they make a move. There is always opposition to anything.

When the ante was upped, there is a response in kind.

Chapter 16

▼

Months passed and nothing happened with the lawyer that was "processing" his papers. Peter drove up to Berserkeley to see the lawyer at BALA, Kurt Sanderson.

"Then, we'll just continue then..."

"What will you do?" Peter asked.

"Well, we'll just continue here, on this end."

"What will you do—what legal moves will you make?"

"I've told you that as long as you see Dr. Williams, we will continue to help you."

"What exactly have you done to help me?"

"We arranged for a lawyer and a doctor to help you."

"What do you mean? What are they doing?"

"I'm not sure I want to continue with this discussion."

"I have explained to you that I am in a dangerous situation. I know too much. I think they are going to try to pick me off. I have been subjected to violent attack.... I was nearly blown up in my car by a federal agent...."

"We want you to see Dr. Williams about that."

"Why? You see, you don't believe me. I showed you proof that my last teaching job was sabotaged. *They* have got to you, too. You believe the other side. You are supposed to be lawyers. You are supposed to uphold the law."

"We are also officers of the court...."

"What is that supposed to mean?"

"We cannot bring frivolous actions. We are duty bound to report to the court wrong doing...."

"So, you are reporting me to the Court?"

"No, but we are keeping them off your back."

"Who is *they*?"

"The little men in black suits."

"They aren't so little...."

"Do you feel that you're being followed?"

"I don't know. I don't think so. But they know where I am. They know how to find me. My car is easy to spot. Maybe there is a beacon on it."

"A beacon?"

"An electronic homing device. It's a small box that sends a radio signal and is attached with a magnet."

"Are you being persecuted?"

"*Yes*! You're damn right...." He said it in despair. He saw that he was being treated as a mental case. The whole program of psychiatric assault and labeling people perfected in Russia had been transplanted to America, and it worked. Maybe he was the experiment, like the government experiment—to control whole towns such as Rangely, Maine, or Mendocino, California. The Human Potential Movement was just a cover.... The Orgon Box provided the cover for what was really going on. Any handy fruitcake with a theory or a religion was used as cover by those who had another agenda.

Any movement was subverted by the very people it stood against. One day the leaders, if they weren't government agents co-opting the movement from the start, even creating it, woke up to the fact that they were bought and paid for. They were blackmailed, controlled, ruined, even killed.

"When people are paranoid," Peter said, "there is usually a good reason for it, according to Freud." He didn't know if Freud said that or not, but it was worth trying out on the man.

"What do you think of the lawyer I provided for you?"

"I don't know. I don't trust him."

"Why not? He's very respected."

"He wanted me to take a false identity. I will not do that. I've done nothing wrong. I am the victim here."

They had said to him: *You will never be published again. We can play pretty rough.*

"I don't want to change my name. That's a hell of a thing for a lawyer to say. I've done nothing wrong. I can't live a lie. I am the victim here."

It was as Kafka described it in *The Trial*.

"We want to release you from the legal problems so that you can write. That's what you want to do, isn't it? Write?"

"What about human rights violations in the United States? A lot of things are happening to a lot of people here, and no one cares. No one can or will do anything."

"We care."

"I don't believe you. Writing is a kind of aberration to you, isn't it? Why should I write any more, if there is no hope of publishing? They said to me "*You will never be published again. We can play pretty rough.*"

"I think you are a good writer."

"What will you do when I leave here now?" What will they do to help me, Peter questioned.

"We'll just continue here. In the meantime, we'd like you to see Dr. Williams and he'll help you with welfare and so on...."

"I told him that I did not want welfare. I do not want to be controlled by anyone. I want a job. I have my own doctors. I am not interested in Dr. Williams. I don't like him and could never relate to him. You have lied to me," Peter said, quietly, the hurt showing in his eyes. His face was contorted with pain and sorrow. "You told me that you wanted me to go see this doctor once to see if I could sustain a suit to try to restore my career. It is apparent that you want me to just talk to him and you will do nothing for me. Who put you up to it? The government? Why are you trying so hard to get me in 'therapy'?"

Peter went away, crying silently. He was a grown man, but he cried more often. He had a big heart and it was gone right out of him.

Kurt Sanderson and the doctor tried to hold Peter there, tried once more to bring him in. They wrote him. Peter did not want to have anything more to do with them, or with their doctor, so called.

> Dear Peter:
>
> I am disappointed by your decision to discontinue the approach suggested by myself, Mr. Sanderson, and Dr. Williams to your problems with the publishing industry, and others.
>
> As you requested, I have enclosed the documents relating to your case which you had given me when we opened up a case file for you, to the present.
>
> I sincerely wish you the best of luck in your pursuits. I shall consider the case closed for our purposes.
>
> Sincerely,

Don't try to resist, because they'll kill you—mentally or spiritually, if not physically.

Civilization has not faced the meaning of its reliance on drugs as a means of controlling social problems.

Once he flew over the Cuckoo's Nest, he was flying pretty low. Sanderson's plan had allowed him to personally assess Peter Casey, but he failed to keep him in their network close. They'd have to use other tactics. Where would Casey surface again?

Chapter 17

▼

Peter went to Monterey to stay. He tried to get a job at Monterey Peninsula College, and returned to see how his application to teach was doing. It had disappeared. They searched the files for days and could not find it. Eventually they said that it had been forwarded to Ft. Ord Army base, of course without asking him. So he figured that Army intelligence was checking him.

Then he found that all record of his ever having taught at Harvard had disappeared from the school. That file was gone too. His files, he discovered, were disappearing everywhere.

He was becoming a non-person.

Peter found that wherever he went, people were checking on him and disbelieving him. Many called the company that had black-listed him, and the chill set in. Things started to happen to him.

He fell asleep on the beach at Lover's Point in Pacific Grove one day, and someone pointed him out to the police. A policeman came down and woke him up and asked for identification. The policeman said that a woman's purse had been snatched. The cop took down all the information on Peter's I.D. Then the woman came over and said, "That's not him!"

Phew!

He met a writer for the local paper and took to talking with him at breakfast in Carmel. The reporter had a girlfriend—a sort of creepy lady named Janet who looked and talked like a duck. She worked for the Secret Service now and then, and the reporter had connections with Army intelligence in Monterey. The whole area was a military colony. Peter didn't find out who these people were connected with until much later. Eventually he saw a photograph of the lady with President Nixon. She belonged to some phoney social register or other.

Peter had no place to stay and no job. Janet offered to put him up for a few nights. She seemed very enthusiastic about him and got him to take her around to some bars. "I've never met anyone who knew so much about the assassination of President Kennedy!" she enthused. "Can I do an interview with you?" Meanwhile, she found out all of his haunts, bars and friends, and set him up. He spilled out all that was happening to him. This screwball seemed pleased, but he was so dense it went right by him. He needed friends.

"For what?"

"For a paper back East that I write for."

He was in poor shape then, and was just a football being passed back and forth.

Peter was lonely and needed friends. So he let her do it, and spent the next couple of weeks answering many questions about his background. They found out everything about him they needed to know. Then one night he went to her friend's house for a drink. As the time passed, the photographer asked more and more questions, never stopping, and Peter began drinking more and more. He pressed relentlessly, ungluing Peter, who was never too stable anyway. It was an interrogation. Peter felt rotten, felt sorry for himself. He wanted to drink and be left alone, wanted to escape, wanted to have a little fun.

But Ben seemed a little sinister. It wasn't anything that Peter could easily put his finger on.

"Do you have anything to eat?"

"I just cooked these two potatoes," Ben told him. "Here, have one."

"I'll eat anything, I'm so hungry."

"That's what I figured...."

"Thank you." He said, taking the foil wrapped potato, unwrapped and started eating it with his fingers.

"May I take a look at your evidence?" Ben said.

"Sure."

Peter ate the potato. From the moment he ate it, he was in trouble. He could not breathe properly. "I've got to go," he said.

"I bet you do…Why don't you go down to the Matador and meet Janet. I'll be there after awhile, as soon as my wife goes to bed. Fresh air will revive you."

"Janet isn't at home?" He was staying with her.

"No."

"Well, I can't get in. I don't have a key." Peter had not a dream in the world what was coming that night.

"Meet her at the Matador."

"Okay. Thanks for the evening."

He went to the bar and found Janet. She was sitting with a creep straight out of the "Godfather."

"My name is Peter," he said, introducing himself. "What's yours?"

"Nick."

"What do you do?"

"I make porno movies. You know. Hard core."

"Does he really?" Peter asked Janet, a bit incredulous that she would be sitting with somebody like that. "Did you just meet this guy or do you know him?"

"I know him. I've never seen any of his films, but I'd like to sometime, just for the thrill!" Well, she was daffy!

"Let me have the key to the house, will you? I want to go to sleep. I don't feel very well. I'm exhausted."

"I misplaced the key. I'm going to meet my son at Sambos when this place closes and he'll let us in. Come on, stay, and have a drink first."

He had one drink. Peter was reeling from too much booze…In addition, there was something about that potato! He felt drugged. It had happened to him before, being fed knockout drops and such.

The bar closed. "We'll meet you there." He was all but blacked out and never quite got to the late night restaurant. The police stopped him a block from Sambos, on an untraveled road. He was weaving across the road, and driving very slowly, about ten miles an hour. Peter should not have been driving, and was totally polluted. It wasn't as though he was on a well traveled road or a freeway. There were no cars around there.

"Let's see your driver's license," the California Highway Patrolman said. He showed it to them. "Walk this line," the officer ordered. He could not walk it very well, or balance on one foot. They arrested him. He was cuffed hard, although docile as a lamb, that he could not use his right hand for months. "Not so hard," he said. "Why do you have to do it so hard?' So he would remember what this was about when he sobered up.

There was no answer. When they got him to the station, they found an excuse to try to beat him up. He was asked to empty his pockets, which he did. He pointed to his medicine. "I have to have that," he said, pointing to his inhalator.

"What?"

"The medicine—" and he reached for his puffer, a "Bronchometer." They got out their sticks and hurled him across the cement floor to a corner, and had started to let him have it when another policeman came in. The beating stopped.

They threw him into a cold cell, where he went into hypothermia, and began shivering violently. He was desperately cold. There were not enough blankets. He could barely breathe without his inhalator. He could have died. Some do die soon after arrest, and it has to be covered up.

They threw someone else into the cell who called the jailer. "Hey, this guy is freezing to death." They brought a number of blankets, and after a couple of hours, he warmed up.

Peter was sure that he had been drugged. He knew The Bottle too well for what had happened to have happened to him quite the way it did. This was new. It must have been something in the potato, since Ben made such a production out of it.

They let him go at dawn, and he walked the long way over the hill from Monterey to Carmel Valley to get his car. It was a nice walk at dawn, although he felt like hell. When he got to his car, it had been gone through. The papers dealing with the evidence brought back from Dallas had been taken.

Ben, the man who fed him the potato had wanted to see that material, so it was in the car when he started out. Why was he showing it to him? He went to the hospital to have his hand X-rayed. His temperature was 2 degrees below normal, even then.

There was a "trial". Peter had never had any kind of ticket before. He had a perfect driving record. He was convicted of drunk driving and paid a fine. He truly hated himself for drinking and driving.

His car was his home. He lived out of it, like a Gypsy. Perhaps, if the thing had been planned, they intended to deprive him of his license or his car.

He walked a thin line of degradation and might end up in the gutter. One foot was in it all too often.

No one would hire him for a real job. He was just barely alive. He wasn't well enough to hold most jobs very long, anyway, but obliterating himself with booze was only going to make it much worse.

The only joys were long solitary hikes in the forest in Big Sur, and even there he was afraid to go since the Forest Service employee tried to blow him up. Afraid he would be seen by the wrong people.

In the camps in the forest, he sometimes met decent people, and for a day or two, the time passed in pleasant conversation. The forest was pure and uncorrupted. It was surrounded by enemies, and threatened with fire, but the streams were pure, the air clean, the swimming good, and the women were naked in the streams and pools in sunshine and shade from the trees.

The camps beside the cool, sweet water of the stream every few miles after a hard hike and climb on the trail were a little bit of paradise.

The fireside at night made everything all right.

Chapter 18

"We have sacrificed reality to words and delivered up our people to the ravenous appetites of the strong. Liberal, democratic ideology, far from expressing our concrete historical situation, disguised it, and the political lie established itself Constitutionally. The moral damage it has caused is incalculable: It has affected profound areas of our existence. We move about in this lie with complete naturalness."

—Octavio Paz

There was stunning news in the papers. In the Fall of 1976, Congress set up a special committee to investigate the assassination of President Kennedy. It was time to try again in the East. To go home and see his parents.

Then something at last came through for Peter. It flowed out of his research. People in San Francisco had heard him speak on the radio, and they arranged for him to receive press credentials to the Congressional Committee in Washington.

He drove back East and wrote stories about the Committee. He was not paid a salary and would have to support himself, but at least it was a start.

They gave him a check for each story that was accepted, but the sum did not come to a lot. Not enough to live on.

In his naivety, it did not immediately occur to him that he'd eventually reap a new whirlwind for this. In only three months, an effort was made to drive him away. But soon, they were all driven away. The first Chairman retired and the second, Henry Gonzales, was greatly feared and was forced out. Henry had been with JFK in the motorcade in Dallas when he was shot. He spent a great deal of time with Peter schooling him in what was going on, and the truth about 1963. The Committee retreated into secrecy after five or six months of sensationally futile activity and counterproductive publicity.

Something was accomplished behind the scenes. Interviews were conducted which could have revealed more of the truth, but this was hidden for sixteen years after they closed up shop, just as the Warren Commission kept secret so much of their work. The implications of what the medical witnesses said was simply too enormous to reveal or properly pursue. It meant that the autopsy report was partially a lie, and that the medical evidence and much more was manufactured. Forged. Fake. Nobody dared say it even if they guessed what it all meant.

It was just too enormous.

The tendency for many was to put their hopes in the Congress, and many expended their energy in trying to work with or help the Committee. So much or all of it was for naught.

The House Select Committee on Assassinations was co-opted and rigged from the start, and doomed to failure.

Peter plunged into a new life for awhile. It was different. When he had a moment to think, the mountains and forests he spent so much time in were before his eyes and never very far from his mind. This bearded man attended hearings in the Capitol Building dressed in plaid woollen Pendleton shirts, jeans, and heavy mountain hiking boots, but carrying a new attaché case. Government agents, posing as newsmen, filmed the odd ball from head to foot, standing close. "Bizarre, aren't I?" he asked one.

"You can say that again!"

Right off the bat he met Lisa, a fine young woman just out of college and had a torrid love affair and wanted to marry her. He lived with an old friend in a small row house in an old part of the city near the waterfront, and made love to the wonderful wench on a mattress on the floor. A wonderful part of it was the wood burning stove in the room, and in the dead of winter the greatest thing in the world was to lie there naked with Lisa in his arms and hear the crackle of the fire and see it through the glass of the stove's door, and listen to great classical music.

For a little while in their lives, in the winter of 1976 and 1977, they were in heaven, before his life became rougher again. It would get much worse.

Peter made the mistake of telling Lisa all about California and couldn't stop talking about—showing her many photos of the interior wilderness of Big Sur. It became her dream. She eventually left the East for San Francisco, then years later made her way to Big Sur where she and her husband remodeled a house in the mountains very close to where Peter had been hiking and taking the photos of the back country which he'd shown her so long before, and a mile or so from where he returned to live and caretake some land. For several years they did not know that fate had brought them so close again until he finally discovered her in 2004. The story is told in "Camping Out," the sequel to this book, though just a small part of the whole story.

In 1979, almost two years after hard times began again, the House Select Committee on Assassinations issued its final report and a dozen volumes on the assassinations of Martin Luther King and President John F. Kennedy. Peter was probably the only researcher who did not immediately dry up and blow away at least for a time, and instead went into instant action: within two weeks or so he was in Dallas and showed the doctors and nurses who had tried to save Kennedy that terrible day in 1963, a copy of the autopsy photo of the back of JFK's head. From that moment on he had the beginnings of the biggest story in our history, and a lot more trouble.

The official photo was seriously altered.

The End

AUTHOR'S BIOGRAPHY
Best Selling Author Harrison Livingstone

This autobiographical novel, *Highway 101*, tells the story of the author's life leading up to 1976 and the sudden establishment of the House Select Committee on Assassinations (HSCA). The Author had been a student of the assassination of President John F. Kennedy, and conducting his own investigation, starting with certain inside information from the FBI, for many years. This led to a major breakthrough engineered by Livingstone as soon as the Committee closed up in 1979, and major trouble due to the competition of negative researchers who had much to lose if Livingstone's evidence held up, as it exposed their work as fraudulent.

His work was later (much later!) extensively corroborated by the Assassination Records Review Board (ARRB) under President Clinton, whose work is presented extensively in Mr. Livingstone's 1998 edition of *High Treason*, his first best seller, and later amplified in *The Radical Right and the Murder of John F. Kennedy* in 2004.

Harry Livingstone grew up with major medical problems since birth and was unable to undertake much physical activity due to an extreme form of asthma. At the age of fourteen he announced that he would become a writer, and that he did, though it took a long time to publish his first novel. Also, as a teenager, along with having been introduced by his father to great writers, he read about President Theodore Roosevelt, a beautiful writer himself about the great American West, and in those writings was the admonition to other asthmatics to undertake the outdoor life as a means of gaining strength and conquering asthma—at least to some extent. There was little means to successfully treat asthma until recently.

Livingstone began going on camping trips as a teenager living alone, and walked and bicycled as much as possible to strengthen his body. Running was out of the question. In his twenties he discovered overnight back-packing and also found the Los Padres National Forest in Big Sur. The experience of losing the trail, described in *Big Sur and the Canyon* (2005), after several days of overland hiking was his first major hike anywhere, and it was in the Monterey County district of the Los Padres' Ventana Wilderness. Ever since, he was a volunteer clearing trail, cleaning camps, and leading others on their first experience of the interior back country.

This book flows from a great trauma in his life in 1971, and is one of two of his outdoor or adventure stories, the other being *The Wild Rose*, a powerful suspense novel set on a ship at sea, which some feel is on a level with Jack London. Perhaps this is also true of *Big Sur and the Canyon*.

Livingstone was a great admirer of President Kennedy, and in shock, traveled to Dallas in December, 1963, shortly after JFK was assassinated, and took a room near Dealey Plaza and began his life-long extraordinary investigation to learn the truth—finding powerful evidence of a conspiracy, along with the discovery of the forgery and fabrication of the autopsy report and photographs, the Zapruder film, and other evidence.

Livingstone has researched the case ever since, producing six major books (several of them best sellers) with a specialty in the medical evidence. His published articles would fill a seventh book. At times his investigative team involved nearly 100 people spanning the nation. In 1979, he was the first person to show copies of the autopsy photographs to the Dallas doctors and nurses and elicited their responses which Penn Jones, Jr. published. The Dallas medical witnesses uniformly denounced the pictures as not representing the wounds they saw. This startling finding has been substantiated by major government investigations involving the autopsy doctors, photographers, corpsmen, and the FBI agents present, as well as other researchers—presented in his books.

His work changed the entire course of the investigation. Questions about the credibility of the medical and photographic evidence were a great taboo, and he had to overcome the "gatekeepers", whose agenda was to insist that the medical and photographic evidence was authentic, whereas Mr. Livingstone held (like the evidence against Lee Harvey Oswald) that it was fabricated. "*All* of the evidence in the case is false!" he says. His task was to prove it, and that he did in his books. Although controversial, he is considered the principal researcher, investigator and writer in the case. Many feel that a great debt is owed him for his work.

He had suspicions for many years about the Zapruder film and those who placed great credibility in it, but "it was very difficult to find something to hang one's hat on" he says. Slowly, the picture came together and he developed powerful evidence of the falsification of even that famous film, presented in *The Hoax of the Century: Decoding the Forgery of the Zapruder Film.*

Mr. Livingstone writes novels, short stories, plays and films. He has written a ballet film for children and their families, feature films, historical dramas about Cortés, Hitler, and the entire American Revolution, and an Elizabethan bawdy comedy. With roots on both coasts of the U.S., he lives in California.

978-0-595-38771-7
0-595-38771-3

Made in the USA
Lexington, KY
18 March 2019